The Vampire

Books by the Same Author

THE DARK MIRROR
NIGHT FROST
NO FLOWERS FOR THE GENERAL
SCRATCH ON THE DARK
DIE NOW, LIVE LATER
DON'T BLEED ON ME
THE MARBLE ORCHARD
DEAD FILE
NO LETTERS FROM THE GRAVE
THE BIG CHILL
STRONG-ARM

Short Stories

NOT AFTER NIGHTFALL
FROM EVIL'S PILLOW

The Vampire

IN LEGEND, FACT AND ART

BASIL COPPER

A Citadel Press Book
Published by Carol Publishing Group

First Carol Publishing Group edition 1990

Copyright © 1973 by Basil Copper

A Citadel Press Book
Published by Carol Publishing Group

Editorial Offices
600 Madison Avenue
New York, NY 10022

Sales & Distribution Offices
120 Enterprise Avenue
Secaucus, NJ 07094

In Canada: Musson Book Company
A division of General Publishing Co. Limited
Don Mills, Ontario

Queries regarding rights and permissions
should be addressed to : Carol Publishing Group,
600 Madison Avenue, New York, NY 10022

Carol Publishing Group books are available at special discounts
for bulk purchases, for sales promotions, fund raising, or
educational purposes. Special editions can also be created to
specifications. For details contact: Special Sales Department,
Carol Publishing Group, 120 Enterprise Ave., Secaucus, NJ 07094

Manufactured in the United States of America
ISBN 0-8065-1126-5

10 9 8 7 6 5 4 3 2

For John Hale, Peter Haining
and August Derleth: who gave
me my first real chances in print

" It will have blood "

William Shakespeare (*MACBETH*)

Contents

𝔍llustrations

Picture Credits

Gerald McKee: 1, 2, 4, 7, 12; Mander and Mitchison Collection:
3; Houston Rogers: 5; Universal Pictures: 8, 9; Hammer Films:
10; Radio Times: 11.

Acknowledgements

My grateful thanks are due firstly to Carl Routledge, who suggested this book and bullied me into writing it; my publisher, John Hale, who enthusiastically undertook to publish it; Gordon Chesterfield, for the care and patience he has put into its production; David Edwards and Gerald McKee, friends and fellow members of the Vintage Film Circle, who gave me valuable advice and suggestions on the chapters relating to the vampire theme in the cinema; Gerald McKee again for the magnificent stills he created for the book; David Lee, for allowing me to view his rare complete print of *Nosferatu*; Peter Haining for advice and suggestions; Raymond Huntley for his courteous and helpful recollections of first creating the role of Dracula on the English stage; Hammer Films, Universal Pictures and private collectors for the loan of stills and other illustrations; Jane Hammond, who typed the manuscript and fought her way patiently and with good humour through the thickets of corrections; and my wife, who has lived with vampires in the house for so long.

In addition, I should like to thank particularly: Messrs. William Hodge and Company Ltd. of London and Edinburgh for their permission to quote passages from their volume, *The Trial of John George Haigh*; Mr. John Gold, editor of the *London Evening News*, Mr. Barry Simmons and Harmsworth Publications Ltd. for permission to quote from their *Evening News* articles on Vampire Hunts in Highgate Cemetery; and the Hutchinson Publishing Group Ltd. for their kindness in allowing me to quote passages from Dr. Montague Summers's volumes *The Vampire in Europe* and *The Vampire: his Kith and Kin*, and from E. F. Benson's story "Mrs. Amworth".

Basil Copper.
1973

Foreword

It should be noted that *The Vampire* is not intended to be read as a work of solemn scholarship. Indeed, in a field where so much is speculative, obscure and dependent on ancient records and dubious eye-witness accounts, such a book would be a near impossibility.

Yet the subject is such a fascinating one and is returned to at such length by fiction writers and particularly in latter years by film-makers, that it did seem to me to be worthy of a more exhaustive, if popular study, than it had hitherto received.

Most of the weighty volumes which appeared in Victorian times and continued into a period as late as the twenties relied heavily on classical accounts and even on legendary speculation. This sort of material is but lightly touched on in *The Vampire* but where an attested account is worthy of more than a passing glance, I have examined it.

Of more importance perhaps are the modern cases of medical vampirism; there are at least two classics in this field, the first that of Sergeant Bertrand in the nineteenth century; the second within the last twenty-five years, the story of a latter-day monster with an insatiable thirst for blood, that of John George Haigh, who was hanged in the late forties for a series of crimes which shocked post-war England.

It has often been noted that the legend of the vampire is one of the most ancient and terrible of all mankind; that is true but the subject, factual, where the facts can be discovered; legendary, where the story is striking enough; artistic—and here the whole field of literature is wide open—has never before, to my knowledge, been dealt with within the scope of one volume of a popular nature. That is not to say that the subject has not been treated in all seriousness where the issues warrant it, but there is a lighter side to even the most sombre topic and the wilder shores of

Hammer Films and even of the popular press have yielded some unexpected flashes of humour.

From Shakespeare's " It will háve blood ", to the B-picture dialogue of " Count Dracula's got a peculiar thirst! " is not so far a step and where the chill of dread quickens into the uncontrollable laugh is a limbo into which this volume is not afraid to dip.

The vampire is even a part of everyday. The London *Times* twice carried reports within a few weeks of each other, in mid-1969, of factual items in which vampirism was quoted as an occurrence. Both are given verbatim in this book.

The Vampire is intended to appeal to those people who would like as much material as possible on the subject within two covers; to those whose appetite—literary, I hasten to add—might be whetted further and thus be persuaded to turn to such magnificent stories as " For the Blood is the Life " and " Mrs. Amworth "; and finally to those who, like myself, have an insatiable interest in the macabre.

Here's to you; may your blood curdle and may you gain as much pleasure in reading this book as I have had in the writing of it.

BASIL COPPER.
Rouvray, Côte-d'Or.

In Legend

ONE

Justice at the Crossroads

POLAND IN the eighteenth century. Across a freezing landscape ducks etch their vivid V-formations in the evening light. Down at the edge of the marshes, reeds, their stems weighted down with ice, stir uneasily in the bitter wind of sunset. The ruts of farm carts, set like iron in the frozen ground, gleam like steel as the afterglow lingers in the sky.

The clatter of a unit of Polish cavalry, their pennants a-flutter against the far horizon, breaks the melancholy of the silence for a few moments; the riders' breath hangs like mist behind them and a thick steam rises from the flanks of the horses. The patrol passes and the wretched village of timber and thatch houses at the edge of the swamp is again silent.

At the edge of the swamp a peasant girl lies sick in the most tumbledown hut in the village; she is the daughter of the widow Marfa, who blames the swamp-spirits for the illness which has already taken her husband. As the girl appears to get worse the mother goes off to summon medical help.

At about the same time a stranger has arrived in the village; a tall, shabby man with bright green eyes, he is carefully noted by the villagers, who see few travellers in this remote corner. As evening draws on he makes his farewell, passing the bent form of Marfa, the peasant woman in the street. Drawing his cloak about him in the freezing air he presses on out of the village when his attention is drawn by a low cry coming from a hut at the skirt of the marsh. The stranger is about to pass on when the low, piercing cry sounds again. He goes over to the door, lifts the latch and disappears within the hut.

Almost an hour later there is a disturbance in the village; the drinkers at the inn are aroused by noise and shouting. The peasant woman Marfa appears among a group of villagers; they are led by the local physician, whom Marfa had summoned to attend her daughter. The clatter of horses' hooves adds to the confusion; the cavalry are returning. The doctor calls the officer over.

He explains that a stranger has been in the village; a girl has died. The man must be found and held for questioning. The officer salutes and snaps a command and the troopers gallop off through the darkling street.

At the inn, prompted by a draught of strong spirit, Marfa tells her story; she had been to fetch the doctor for her sick daughter. She returned ahead of the physician and found the door of her hut ajar. Her daughter was dying, caught in a tumbled heap of bed-clothes saturated with blood. She was struggling with a strange, tall man with bright eyes who held a shining instrument in his hand. The man had jumped up as Marfa shrieked and after saying something in a tongue she could not make out, ran into the night.

The doctor had arrived some time later to find his patient beyond earthly help. In his opinion the girl had died of the same disease as her father but he had to admit that there were scratches on the throat and blood issuing from the wounds; but these might well have been caused naturally with the sores breaking with neck movement during her death-struggles. There are mutters of " The undead ", from some of the more superstitious peasants gathered round and the doctor smiles bitterly to himself.

He does not blame these simple people for such thoughts; he has no doubt in his own mind that the flicker of firelight over the tall man's face and the old woman's overwrought state had been responsible for her half-demented condition. He glances round the squalor of the inn parlour with distaste. If only he could divorce these people from their age-old superstitions and inculcate in them some of the simple elements of hygiene. He shakes his head impatiently as Marfa goes on with her maledictions on the monster who has destroyed her daughter.

" The soldiers will soon bring him back," says the doctor crossly.

Presently the horsemen return, bringing with them the tall figure of the stranger; he is tied with a spare set of reins and has been forced to run behind the captain's horse. He is pale, his cloak covered with mud and his green eyes glow balefully at his captors.

While the captain questions the man in the inn taproom, the remainder of the troop is sent to fetch the magistrate, who lives about ten miles distant. The stranger, it is established, is German and as the captain of cavalry does not understand the language, the physician himself takes over the examination. The man's name, it transpires, is Sebastian Moeller; he comes from Munster and is travelling to Warsaw on business as an apothecary. He maintains, despite close questioning, that he was attempting to administer medical assistance to Marfa's daughter. There is laughter at this as the doctor translates the reply and the captain spits loudly upon the floor.

The arrival of the magistrate, in an unpleasant temper at being aroused from his dinner, interrupts the proceedings and he orders Moeller to be locked in a cellar. He then goes into a private conversation with the captain and the doctor. The three retire to an inner room and the magistrate begins to make copious notes of the doctor's interrogation. He sends for Marfa and listens to her story before dismissing her and the remaining peasants to their homes. He finds a *prima facie* case against the prisoner and announces his intention of bringing Moeller to trial the following afternoon.

He clatters back to his mansion within half an hour, escorted by the captain and his troop; the doctor rides homeward, thinking bitterly of the high-handed manner of magistrates. Marfa lies in her hut, her grief blunted by drink. Her daughter is still, her hands composed across her breast, her shadow dancing against the ceiling in the last flickering of the fire.

The stranger draws his cloak about him in the dampness of the cellar and desperately searches for a way out; there is none and he sits down on a barrel to grimly await the morning.

The trial takes up most of the afternoon of the following day and it is almost dusk before the verdict is announced. The proceedings are held at the inn, which is jammed to the doors. The stranger stands in chains before the magistrate. The defendant is not allowed to contradict the witnesses and most of the proceedings are not translated for him.

It is obvious that the magistrate has already decided on Moeller's guilt. He runs through the questions and answers already elicited by the physician in a most perfunctory way and appears to be asleep for the greater part of the afternoon, though he occasionally opens his eyes sharply when Moeller dares to speak in his own defence. Once he threatens to have the prisoner gagged if he makes any more interruptions.

Moeller has regained some of his composure now and stands, a forlorn and yet defiant figure, his shoulders thrown back and his chest rising and falling with his rapid breathing. His cloak hangs in threadbare elegance from his long form and his greenish eyes are fixed unblinkingly on the coarse face of the magistrate. Now and again the physician condescends to translate a sentence for him. In the doctor's pouch is the small lancet for blood-letting he has recovered from the floor of the hut; if it would support the defendant's case he appears oblivious of the fact for he had not brought it to the magistrate's attention and it is evident that if he did its significance would escape that gentleman's intelligence.

The day is dwindling into dusk and the lamps have been brought in before the prisoner is allowed to testify on his own behalf. He speaks in a strong voice, occasionally interpolating a halting phrase in Polish.

" Christ be my witness, I only went to the girl's aid, as any man with the healing art would do; I call on God and these good people here assembled to send me from this company an innocent man," the doctor translates finally.

There is a tremble of amazement round the room and the magistrate, awakening hastily from a wine-induced stupor calls harshly for silence. He keeps his eyes fixed somewhere over the prisoner's head as he pronounces sentence. He is already thinking of his supper. He sentences Moeller to death as " a creature of evil and perverted ways ". Execution would take place immediately. Moeller bows mockingly to the court and is led off by the troopers. The physician and the magistrate march out to the coach waiting in front of the tavern. The lancet rattles against the loose coins in his pouch as the doctor descends the steps.

The dying sun stains the marshes redly and ice glistens in the potholes as the procession arrives at the crossroads. The horses of the cavalry slip and slither on the rutted way; the magistrate's equipage follows behind, containing the owner and the physician. Moeller walks behind the carriage, a rope from his wrists secured to the back axle. He looks neither left nor right and retains a measure of tattered dignity. Immediately behind him rides the captain, supervising the prisoner's guard.

Then follows a great procession of peasants, almost every man, woman and child in the village; prominent among them is Marfa, whose eyes speak hatred for the prisoner with every glance she directs at his back. Arrived at the crossroads, the peasants form up in a hollow square with a great tree as one of its corners, while the magistrate descends from his carriage. This man, who is to write in his report later that evening, " This day we safely destroyed a demon," looks incuriously at the prisoner. A chill wind whistles among the branches of the leafless tree; the light is rapidly going from the sky. The side lamps of the carriage are lit and the beams of lanterns begin to prick the gloom at the edges of the crowd.

" Let the sentence be carried out," orders the magistrate.

A strong rope has already been thrown over the branch of the tree; a noose sways gently in the wind. Moeller is dragged over towards the tree and the lead-rope removed from his hands. He stands with the noose about his neck, his green eyes staring with a curious fire at the crowd greedy for sensation.

Then his lips move silently as he glances skywards. The physician shifts uneasily from his position beside the carriage; if the thought were not blasphemous one might imagine that the prisoner was offering a prayer. Then a trooper claps spurs to his horse's flanks, the beast leaps forward and the rope attached to its saddle begins to sing and creak over the high branch. The prisoner's feet leave the ground with a jerk, kick convulsively for a minute or so and are then still. The crowd sighs with satisfaction; Moeller's body hangs limply.

Five minutes pass before the magistrate orders him to be taken down; he confers with the physician and the captain. As the rope is unloosed from round the executed man's neck the village butcher steps forward; he is one of the biggest men in the hamlet and his forearms, thick with muscle, show like red meat themselves under the frayed sleeves of his jerkin.

He carries his largest axe over his shoulder; two of the troopers drag Moeller forward over the frozen ground. The axe describes an arc and bites dully into flesh and bone; the butcher swears and tries again. It takes three blows before the head is severed from the body. While the sharpened stake is produced soldiers throw torches into the bonfire of brush and timber which has been prepared on the magistrate's orders earlier in the afternoon.

The remainder of the cleansing work is soon done and justice has been upheld once again in the remote places of the kingdom. When Moeller's body has been impaled, the stake firmly through its heart, both corpse and head are hurled into the middle of the roaring fire.

Then and only then do the villagers, released as though from some trance-like state, begin to wheel and dance about the blazing pyre, warming their hands as they bob and circle. The magistrate, his fat face even more pink in the light from the reflected fire, accepts the doctor's congratulations. The captain canters up to make his report.

The physician thanks the magistrate for his gracious offer of conveyance back to the village and the carriage rumbles off, the flames re-echoed redly from its sides. One by one the villagers slip away as the flames die, until only Marfa is left. The troopers remain on each side of the great fire until it begins to cool. Then they too clatter back towards the dark hamlet and the crossroads are once again given over to the night. In the magistrate's carriage the physician quietly takes Moeller's lancet from his pouch; his companion is sleeping by his side. The doctor quickly hurls the knife out of the window.

The bonfire hisses and spits as it gradually dies, dust and ash is scattered by the searching wind which springs up, and the ducks fly out over the marshes, their V-formations almost invisible against the massing clouds. Marfa walks back toward the village, her thin shoulders hunched against the bitter wind. The night of bigotry once again settles across the land.

The flames which consumed Moeller were symptomatic of thousands of similar fires which were lit at countless crossroads all over Europe and in many other parts of the world for many centuries. And crossroads were the unvarying venue in matters which dealt with the undead. The Polish example is typical of many such cases of bigoted cruelty which could be quoted to support the theme of this book; a theme which was often the pretext for blind rage, sadism and revenge.

Though practice might vary from country to country, the beliefs of many peoples in former times associated the place where two or more roads crossed with witchcraft, wizardry, magic and all manner of evil practices. And it was felt that summary justice, as in Moeller's case, particularly fitted the monstrous practices thought to be indulged in by all manner of evildoers.

In England, for hundreds of years, it was the practice to bury the bodies of those who had committed suicide at crossroads, and usually a stake was driven through the corpse's heart. In the early nineteenth century a law was passed in England under which the body of a person who had committed suicide was bound to be buried privately between 9 p.m. and midnight and no religious ceremony was permitted. This barbaric statute was removed as late as 1882 and from then onwards all such restrictions have been void.

The particular relevance of the crossroads to suicide was that in ancient times it was believed that people who had taken their own lives walked as ghosts at the crossroads until their bodies could be recovered and buried in a graveyard with all the rites of Christianity. That being impossible with suicides, a stake was driven through their bodies in order to keep their ghosts from wandering abroad at night.

This idea was undoubtedly the basis of the belief that driving a stake through the corpse of the undead dead was efficacious in destroying its ability to walk abroad again; certainly the practice was widely spread by the Middle Ages. Another strong reason for selecting a crossroads for the interment and execution of a being who might again walk by night was an eminently practical one.

Authorities argued in those far-off times that if a ghost or demon issued from the grave and if that grave stood at a cross-roads, the apparition would then find four footways stretching out in different directions before it. In which case it would be perplexed in knowing which path to take and might remain there undecided until dawn, when it would be compelled to return to the earth. But there was great danger for any unfortunate person who might chance to venture that way after dusk when the demon was standing undecided at the junction of the four ways. So this in turn led all sensible people to shun crossroads after dark, taking the view that there were no places more witch-haunted or cursed.

Another common practice was to erect the gallows at a cross-roads, where the hangman's victim rotted in chains, swaying, a melancholy figure in the wind at sunset.

Witches too were associated with crossroads, particularly in former times in places like Wales, where they were presumed to spend their days under rocks and stones near crossroads and creep out to steal children after dusk. Here also, at this cursed and magical place, grew the mandrake, the plant which screamed like a human being when plucked and was a symbol of fertility.

It will be remembered that in both the Goethe and Marlowe versions of Faust, the physician made his infamous bargain with the Devil after reading in his forbidden books that to conjure up Mephistopheles one had merely to call upon him thrice at any crossroads. And the crossroads was a vital ingredient of the famous scene in which the apparition appeared.

Even in the East the crossroads had a horrifying reputation and in India she-devils were reputed to drink the blood of elephants that ventured upon a place where four ways came together.

There are many classic examples of these beliefs in Russia also, where the legends of the undead dead have been kept alive for many centuries. In this vast and still primitive country where legends die hard, in the more remote areas of the many nations which make up the U.S.S.R., the crossroads has particular horror in that it is reputedly the favourite rendezvous of the animated corpse. Here the foul thing lurks on the outlook for some unsuspecting traveller in these lonely places and if an unfortunate does pass that way he or she is strangled and devoured, the monster drinking the blood of his victim.

The undead dead are particularly feared at Christmastime when they make the crossroads their meeting place, and even in civilised England the legend of the witches gathering at lonely road junctions in remote country areas to hold their sabbats is not entirely lost today. The spirits of the dead are presumed to gather at the crossroads in Germany also and there are many striking legends extant and examples handed down by word of mouth through the country folk.

The crossroads which is situated near a cemetery is particularly feared and haunted in many countries which still retain their primitive beliefs and superstitions. People who are in dread that the dead may return to prey upon the living are conversely comforted by the fact that the crossroads may act in " detaining " undead spirits in the manner already described. But the route between the crossroads and the cemetery would be a doubly haunted place in that case, with the spirits of the undead being " trapped " between the two localities.

The atmosphere, even today, of a lonely country crossroads at sunset makes it easy to see why people of an earlier age should associate the conjunction of such remote by-ways with evil spirits of the undead. The wind sighs uneasily in the branches; black clouds scud across the sky; the long fingers of the departing light throw blood-red patterns across the ground. The harsh noise of bare branches and brittle grass stems rubbing together raise prickles on the spine and the freezing air engenders an equal chill of the spirits. A thin mist rises from the blue woodland as the sun departs and the spirits of unseen, intangible things with evil intent seem to ride the skirts of the wind.

It is not difficult to understand, even in this twentieth century, why primitive peoples, reared in ignorance and darkness, should stir uneasily at their firesides at any passing shadow, while even the creaking of a farm-cart, its wheels grating over the frozen ruts at dusk, could hold sinister import for the startled peasantry at the chimney corner.

The sophisticated too, as we have seen, were not immune from the black terrors of nightfall; terrors that flourished long before the age of electricity and urbanisation and which seemed to breed prejudice and cruelty in equal measure. Indeed, as has been observed in other fields, the more sophisticated a man and the more subtle his mind, the greater his cruelty and prejudice when opportunity offered. The present study will afford many instances of this.

Let us take another example of justice at the crossroads, this time from Hungary, for long centuries regarded as the classic haunt of the undead and a land where the extraordinary is commonplace. This concerned a man called Huebner, who died about 1725. The district where he lived became a plague-spot in which local people were attacked at night in mysterious circumstances and large numbers of cattle were killed.

When this had gone on for a year or two and no one had been apprehended—no one in fact, who was attacked, had even caught a glimpse of the face of the person assaulting him, so cunningly had the marauder gone about his business, approaching stealthily from behind, at night and usually in remote areas of thick woodland—the people of the neighbourhood began to whisper that the undead was responsible.

Many of the attacks were in the vicinity of the cemetery where Huebner's corpse had been interred. This factor, combined with another, made the authorities suspicious. The person making the attacks, particularly on the cattle, was evidently a person of enormous strength, because the animals had been strangled. Huebner in life had been a man of giant size, celebrated for his strength and the power of his hands. The whole district became so uneasy about this that the magistrate deputed to look into the affair eventually ordered that the body of Huebner should be disinterred.

What they found was startling and terrifying indeed: Huebner's body bore all the classic marks of the undead. The body was taken to the public gallows, at a crossroads, and there decapitated by the local executioner. The corpse, with a stake through the breast, together with the head, was thrown on to an enormous bonfire built at the crossroads and burned to ashes. Later the ashes themselves were scattered to the wind. Even corpses of people buried near the cursed Huebner were cremated and then reinterred. Once again justice had been dispensed at the crossroads.

Fire has traditionally been associated with disposal of the undead and the cremation of the animated corpse usually took place at the junction of several roads, where the public gibbet often stood. An interesting association of fire with the " wasting disease " of the undead comes from Germany and also Eastern Europe, where a special ceremony took place in olden times. In many districts cattle were often attacked by a form of anaemia, which took heavy toll of their numbers. The superstitious peasantry—though in this case simple hygiene by way of cleansing through fire might have formed the basis of the practice—instituted a ceremonial lighting of bonfires, to rout the demons lurking within the cattle.

The practice appears to have come down from pagan times and was a common resort of witch covens in the Middle Ages. The procedure was for all ordinary fires in domestic hearths in a town or village to be extinguished. A fire was then lit from friction only —usually by the classic method of rubbing two twigs together— and when this had been built into a sizeable pyre the cattle were ceremonially driven through the smoke and flame. Following this symbolic purgation, all the fires in the village were re-lit by torches kindled at the main pyre. Not surprisingly this method of casting out demons did not prove very efficacious, even when the cattle were driven over the crossroads after passing through the flames.

In Russia there is a similar tradition, though the peasantry there felt simply that the undead were preying on the cattle. In those districts where the plague struck the fires were lit in order that the demon should not pass, for fire was known to be the traditional enemy of the reanimated corpse. France and Poland had corresponding beliefs, and similar ways of dealing with the night-demons which affected the animals with the pernicious wasting disease.

The connection of the undead with the confluence of roads and foot-tracks is also linked in legend and history with suicide. A solitary tree, which became a landmark as generations trudged up and down the rough cart-tracks, often became the focal point of traffic. It was here, in these spots, after nightfall lonely and seldom frequented, that the suicide came to perform his solitary and melancholy task, often by means of a rope suspended from the branches of the tree. This added to the legend too, and the ghost or wandering spirit of the suicide thus became one of the dreaded night-things which walked after dusk. The solitary tree was also pressed into use for summary execution, as we have seen in Moeller's case; and where there was no tree the gibbet was erected in its place. Here corpses rotted month after month, their skins turned to leather by exposure to the weather, their eyes pecked out by crows and other carrion.

Small wonder that the crossroads was a shunned place and that only the strongest-nerved dare venture there after dark. And as the centuries advanced so the legends and the wild tales accrued round the places where roads came together; in time the facts of execution and cruelty became inextricably jumbled with stories and tales of witches and witch covens, demons, spirits of the undead, walkers from nearby cemeteries, and even with the stealthy diseases which attacked healthy cattle and brought them a lingering death.

Of all the demons which inhabited the areas round lonely crossroads none were more feared than the undead. The undead, to medieval man might take many forms; he might be a genie or spirit which rode the night wind. To others he would be a female witch or a warlock, riding abroad on nights of storm and gale, usually glimpsed by the lightning flash, tattered cloak flying in the wind. To some he could be a gaunt, tottering figure, half-glimpsed against some sunset skyline, recently from the graveyard and with the charnel stench about him. Not even the rotting corpse swinging gently in his chains in the rising wind of nightfall was more feared than this last; the haunter of churchyards and corpse-places, whose signalled approach was a sign for bolted doors, invocations of the Deity and the rush to the church altar.

More terrible even than these, the mysterious attacker who reserved his brutal assaults for women and children predominantly; usually near the crossroads and always after nightfall. Even for those who escaped there was no rest and after death he could still reclaim his victim.

The undead dead; the attacker of the old and feeble, particularly in their sleep; the corpse-violator; the haunter of the graveyard; he was all these and more, for he lived beyond the bounds of death.

The name given to this terrible scourge by sophisticated and simple alike was Vampirism.

TWO

It will Have Blood

VAMPIRE! WHAT a dread that name had to people of the ancient world. From the mists of antiquity the term meant an incubus which sustained itself by sucking the life from the living. It was known in Greek and Roman times and seems to have been common to most countries and climates, though the legend flourished most strongly in Eastern Europe during the past three hundred years. Yet the word itself had many connotations as the centuries passed; to those in medieval Europe a vampire was a person of wicked ways who, having died, lived on by feeding on the blood of human beings by which he—or she—sustained immortal life.

In Eastern Europe the term *nosferatu* was used to denote the vampire, which became as dreaded a name as the werewolf with which to frighten naughty children into being good; and elsewhere other terms came into general use. But they all meant one thing: a living-corpse which carried on its unnatural life by feeding on the blood of the living.

With the legend also developed a wealth of detail concerning the creatures: that they could be kept at bay by using certain herbs, notably garlic; that they recoiled from the crucifix, were unable to pass over water; that they slumbered in their coffins by day, only venturing out at dusk, when their unnatural life began; that they cast no reflections in a mirror. Earth from their native land was said to furnish their unnatural bed, within their coffins, where they slumbered in vaults by day, their unearthly life held in suspension until the dusk, when they were released to prowl and seek their victims. The victim of a vampire, attacked as though by a wasting disease, in his turn died and also became a vampire, thus breeding a plague of blood-sucking monsters on the earth. They had, it was said, the ability to change themselves into a wolf or a bat and when they appeared in their victims' rooms at night, they first soothed their fears by stroking movements before plunging their unnaturally long and razor-sharp canine teeth into the victim's throat.

As ages passed the legend was embellished: the vampire could only be killed by driving a stake through his heart—if he could be caught in his coffin during a period of daylight. This seems to have been the most popular and favoured method of disposing of a vampire but there were other procedures, equally efficacious. A vampire's intended victim might escape by wearing a rosary or crucifix round his neck, if he placed garlic or wolfbay before his doors or windows, or if he stood within a circle formed by sprinkling holy water, which the vampire was powerless to cross. Those so protected could then deal with the monster. He could be shot with a silver bullet; a pick could be used to pierce his breast; he could be hanged and the stake then used in the traditional method; or his head could be severed and the remains consumed by fire. According to the age of the vampire he would first commence visibly to decay and, if he were old enough, would literally disintegrate into bones and dust.

There were a number of ways of distinguishing a vampire— notably by the loathsome stench of his breath. Bloodsuckers naturally had a charnel smell about them and one of the results of drinking blood is a type of sickness which is quite distinctive. The vampire was naturally lean, white-faced with piercing eyes—he was also said to have hypnotic powers to overcome his victims— he had elongated and dirty finger nails and of course—a notable distinction—he could also be identified by his long, sharp and pointed teeth, which were impossible to hide.

The legends were embellished by facts of natural history, notably that of the habits of the vampire bat of South America and in such tropical countries as Java and Sumatra which lived by inserting its teeth into creatures it first " hypnotised " by stroking motions; it sucked up the nourishing blood, revitalising itself by this means, leaving its victim to die of anaemic exhaustion.

We shall be meeting the vampire bat again in later chapters

and also a more recently discovered horror, the vampire moth. But revolting though these creatures may be, at least they are natural phenomena. The darker pages of medical history are littered with examples of vampires of the non-supernatural sort: human beings who are walking casebooks, who derive a morbid physical satisfaction by slaking their unnatural thirst by drinking the blood of the living or—even more horrible—of the newly dead. There are several such cases cited in the present volume.

The dictionary defines the term " vampire " as being the " ghost or re-animated body—usually of wizard, heretic, criminal etc.—that leaves [the] grave at night and sucks [the] blood of sleeping persons; person who preys on others ". This is the perfect description of the vampire of classical times and of literature and this is the definition which has come to typify the creature of this study.

But how was one to identify such a creature and what were the characteristics by which he could be distinguished? We have already mentioned the " lean and hungry look ", the sharp and polished teeth, the breath, and the other physical details. Many were the instances in earlier times when graves were opened on suspicion, particularly in Central and Eastern Europe. Historians and scholars particularise the horrible circumstances in which tombs were broached and the monsters exorcised, usually under the direction of priest or bishop.

The dead, far from showing symptoms of decay and, as is usual, having sunken cheeks and long flowing hair, were fresh and undecayed, their cheeks plump and healthy, their bodies sleek and well-nourished, their hair ungrown and with a general air of well-being about them. Some had diabolical smiles on their faces, while others—perhaps most terrible of all—had their eyes fixed and open so that they seemed to be staring at the terrified on-looker and watching his every move.

The creatures were able to materialise and disappear as mist when rising from their graves at dusk and in returning to their hiding places at dawn; some would have evidence of their horrid nightly work about them, usually in the form of blood-traces at the corners of the mouth or—as sometimes happened—when the bottoms of the coffins were aswill with blood. The horror of these circumstances may well be imagined and the vampire has had a terrible power that has come down through the pages of history for the past three thousand years.

There were other ways of dealing with vampires also; if their lair could be detected, holy water could be sprinkled around the resting place and prayers said, which would prevent the creature from returning to its resting place. Or, best of all, the priest or person in authority, could place a crucifix in the coffin within the vault which would prevent the unholy thing from regaining its home. Forced to remain abroad after daylight hours, the vampire would then crumble into dust at the first rays of the rising sun.

Over the years and especially in modern times, the term "vampire" has meant many things to different people. In the twenties of this century vampire usually described an adventuress who leeched on to helpless men and sucked them dry of money and material possessions. With the word shortened to vamp, the cinema of the twenties found a classic example in Theda Bara, an actress who took as her name an anagram of " Arab Death " and who was photographed with skulls and bones to epitomise her victims.

To literary-minded people of the late Victorian age, the vampire meant only one thing: Count Dracula, Bram Stoker's super monster, the satanic hero of a badly-written novel which nevertheless has enough power to enthrall and terrify the reader even today.

To a later generation addicted to short stories of the macabre sort, the vampire meant something else: perhaps Mrs. Amworth, the deadly heroine of E. F. Benson's terrifying study; or possibly the most subtle delineation of a vampiric presence ever created in literature, the Horla of Guy de Maupassant.

From 1931 onwards the vampire was the screen Dracula, the late Bela Lugosi, the former Hungarian cavalry officer turned actor whose spare, saturnine presence, broken accent and sweeping movements created an immortal film character and set a standard which later artistes have attempted to emulate but have never quite been able to equal.

And finally, for millions of people too young to have been nurtured on the original, vampirism was represented during the late fifties, sixties and seventies by Hammer Films' prolific output, with Old Wellingtonian Christopher Lee re-appearing from the grave time after time to stalk the aisles of the Odeons and the Essoldos as the dreadful Count.

It is perhaps easy to smile at some of the manifestations of what has become a latter-day cult; but that there is a serious basis

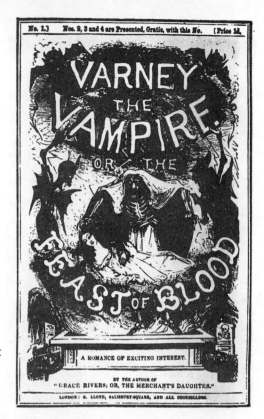

(*right*) The cover of the first vampire serial, *Varney the Vampire*. (*below*) Varney and his victim

(*left*) Bram Stoker. (*below*)
Old and new editions of
famous works by Bram
Stoker

for the legend there can be little doubt for those who have made even the most cursory examination of the phenomena. Shakespeare recognised this when he made Macbeth say, " It will have blood; they say, blood will have blood." It was a vivid sentence which must have struck an uneasy chord in the hearts of his contemporary audiences.

Vampirism as a medical problem is perhaps rare, but far from unknown; the appalling case of John George Haigh, who murdered a number of people in England in the late nineteen-forties and drank their blood, after drawing off quantities from their bodies after death, is too recently in the memory to permit any doubt of this.

And as I indicated in my introduction, newspaper reports of vampirism in which sheep, cattle and even human beings have been attacked, are far from uncommon. What seems lacking is any thorough investigation of the reports and, of course, it is easy to be sceptical when such stories emanate from primitive peoples living in such remote places as Malaya, Burma and the islands of the Pacific.

This book will attempt to list and examine such strange by-passes of the human—and inhuman—and in so doing will uncover many extraordinary and bizarre incidents in a field which may be fresh to many and, without descending too deeply into the morbid, holds much fascination and what one may describe as the poetry of the night.

THREE

The Growth of the Legend

As we have already seen, so powerful was the hold of the vampire and its evil aura on the superstitious mind that many innocent people must have perished on mere suspicion; just as thousands more were to perish in the wave of mass-hysteria which culminated in the notorious witch-trials of the seventeenth century. The witch or warlock, however, has little or nothing in common with the vampire legend and is consequently outside the scope of this work.

No one knows how the legend of the vampire began. It seems common to most countries and to have been taken as absolute truth by ignorant and semi-literate populations at different periods of history. Its origin is lost in the vastness of time. Yet, from all accounts—and records appear to be better authenticated from Roman times onwards—vampires seemed to lie thickest on the ground in places like Russia, Poland and Eastern Europe in general.

Why Eastern Europe—and particularly Transylvania? And in Transylvania why the Carpathians? Just as in dealing with Germany one finds that legends persist in association with the Harz Mountains. Transylvania now lies within the borders of Communist Romania and Communists, one must imagine, would not look too kindly on such spectral emanations. They smack too much of non-conformity.

Yet the legends persist in Eastern Europe, even under the Communist regimes; it may be that in such places as Poland,

Romania, Bulgaria and Russia—territories that have been fought over for centuries by warring factions—the deeds of cruelty that were done, originally by feuding tribes, then by the conquerors who swept across the Slavic borders over hundreds of years, became distorted and twisted as time passed and collective memory became dim.

Where cruelty—and horror was piled upon horror during this period—passes into legend and becomes supernatural terror is problematical; but we may say without fear of contradiction that such deeds have accreted more and more terrifying detail with the passing centuries. So it may well be with the vampire and the wealth of chilling circumstance with which the myth is surrounded.

Before we take a look at the figure of the vampire more closely, we will glance at some of its manifestations as recorded through the lore of ancient peoples.

Blood sacrifice has been the practice of primitive peoples down through the ages and is still common in remote corners of the world today. Small wonder then that the cruel practices of such nations as the Aztecs and the Incas should have given rise to the wilder fantasies of the vampire cult. And the shedding of blood on sacrificial altars was not confined merely to more barbaric civilisations. Sophisticated societies like those of the ancient Egyptians, the Greeks and the Romans offered up the blood of innumerable victims to appease the Fates and gain favour with their dark gods.

Undoubtedly there is a link between these devilish rites and the legend of the vampire; but equally truly the loathsome vitality of the living dead which the vampire represents has been opposed by the Christian church, the shadow of whose crucifix has brought terror to the undead and kept the plague at bay. Just as the vampire was reputed to live on through weary century after century so have the representatives of the church in all parts of the world continually formed the main opposition to the horrors of the undead.

The power of the crucifix has already been mentioned; not only was its shadow feared literally by the vampire but its touch could burn like living coals. On numberless occasions ancient documents have recorded that a crucifix, swiftly produced by priest or cleric and laid on the suspected vampire's skin caused symptoms of burning and left a reddish-black mark such as that induced by scorching.

In Central Europe, where whole villages were laid waste by the scourge and hundreds lived in terror, life could only go on by virtue of the thin, unbreakable line of the priesthood, which was the only tangible authority powerful enough to keep the dread figure of the vampire at bay.

The Catholic Church has been in the vanguard of the struggle against the unholy forces of the undead and ancient superstition alike; in many parts of the world, particularly in ancient times, people born with deformities or mental defects were suspected of possessing devilish propensities or vampiric tendencies. Occasionally whole communities would be overcome by a sort of collective frenzy and dozens of victims perished in holocausts of destruction, the perpetrators believing that they were exterminating literal nests of vampires.

Natural death itself has added to the legend in this instance; during the eighteenth and nineteenth centuries premature burial was a frequent occurrence, due mainly to faulty diagnosis and primitive medical techniques. In cases of catalepsy the unfortunate victim would sometimes be interred while still alive and when the wretch attempted to tear himself out of his coffin or, as sometimes happened, would be found in a digging position when a vault would be opened to inter another member of the same family, this gave further fearful evidence of the truth of the existence of the vampire. Edgar Allan Poe and other celebrated writers often made premature burial the subject of their macabre short stories.

Even in the late twentieth century, despite modern techniques and more enlightened teachings, premature burial is not unknown and a number of potential victims in cataleptic trance or arrested animation have been discovered alive almost on the point of burial or cremation. How could one state categorically, horrible as the supposition may be, that such things do not happen today and remain undetected? In which case there must be thousands of unrecorded cases in past ages which have swelled the legend of the vampire and terrified millions at their firesides.

Legend has linked the vampire in human form with the vampire bat which also ventures out at night, sleeps by day and exists by slaking its thirst on the blood of living creatures; we shall be examining this creature in more detail a little later but it is useful at this stage to remember that the bat is one of the favourite forms in which the vampire appears. So disguised he can flit his way to the bedside of his victim undetected, as dusk falls and once within the window or on the balcony of the house he has chosen, can then restore himself to human form.

We have already mentioned the various herbs and other protective materials with which the victim can guard his life against the loathsome menace, but a bright fire in the room was almost as great a deterrent and must have saved many lives. One of the vampire's greatest fears is that of the elements of fire and water; as we have noted he cannot cross water, though he is able to do so when secreted within a vessel. Fire is even more deadly to him and if his coffin should be destroyed by fire while he is abroad at night, then he is helpless; his home is closed to him and he will dissolve into dust when caught by the advent of daylight.

When the vampire seeks his victim at the bedside he or she will already be drowsy with sleep; the hypnotic power of the vampire's eyes then induces a trance-like state and while caressing kisses of the mouth and throat follow, the vampire's sharp teeth nip swiftly into the neck or throat and the blood is then ingested.

Another curious feature is that little bleeding continues once the vampire has ceased his attack and withdrawn. If the vampire's advances are not prevented—and he will return night after night until he has reduced his victim to a lifeless husk—then the victim once dead will himself become a vampire and prey on others in his turn. As we shall see, this craving for blood can take the form of feasting on small animals, birds, rats and even flies and other insects, failing a human victim.

In Greece in ancient times, when a man or woman died, the family and other close relatives took it in turns to watch all night to see that no evil spirits entered the body; if a cat or dog jumped over the body it was considered that the dead person might well become a vampire.

To guard against the vampire, mustard seed would be spread on the roof of the house and the doors barricaded with brambles and thorny plants. If a vampire appeared, it was believed that he would stop to count the mustard seed and dawn would catch him long before he got to the end of his task. Similarly, if he tried to force his way into the house the brambles would hold him fast. The flight of a bird over a body would also arouse terrible suspicions among the family of the dead person and the corpse would be pierced to kill the vampiric intruder.

In China there is a legend that a cat may impart the tendencies of a vampire to a corpse and this animal is never allowed in a room in which there has been a death; the Chinese believe that if it jumps over the body something of its savage nature will enter into the soul of the dead man. In Japan there is an interesting legend of a vampire cat which we shall be meeting in a later chapter.

The wolf too, was suspect by primitive peoples, and in Greece and some parts of South America, it was said that if a wolf killed a sheep and someone then ate of the sheep he was in danger of becoming a vampire. The wolf, of course, could only be killed by a silver bullet, a fact central to lycanthropy and the legends connected with it.

The great seventeeth-century French philosopher and theologian Dom Augustin Calmet says of the vampire legend, which he regarded as a fact beyond dispute, that for the creation of a vampire, three things were necessary: the vampire, the devil and the permission of Almighty God.

Crossroads also play a great part in the cult of the vampire; in medieval times they were shunned at dusk as they were believed to be haunted and used as a rendezvous by the undead. As we have seen in Chapter One a vampire was often dealt with at a cross-roads and would be beheaded and burnt on that spot, as a form of poetic justice. In later years the crossroads was also used as a site on which to hang miscreants, and a public gibbet often stood at such lonely spots.

Not many records exist of the thoughts and experiences of a vampire's victim; this is usually left to the writer of fiction, who was fond, particularly in Victorian times, of depicting the heroine in the most ghastly situations and at the mercy of a vampire; these attacks were partly sexual in their undertones and may have accounted for the immense popularity of this type of fiction in the late Victorian age. A few authentic accounts exist, however, of people attacked by vampires in Central Europe in the eighteenth century and they all tally to a remarkable degree.

In each case the victim survived to live on without vampiric tendencies, as the monster was disturbed at his work in time to prevent the victim becoming addicted. The accounts speak of terrible dreams suffered by the sleeper; of the "sharp fangs and piercing red eyes" of the demon which overpowered them; of a feeling of sickness and suffocation; of the monster lying along his victim in a sexual posture; of a great weight on the chest; of excessive perspiration.

When the victim awakened from the spell, a scream was sufficient to rouse the family and send the vampire off in headlong flight. The victim's terror may be imagined at awakening under such circumstances, at dead of night, in a darkened chamber and finding himself or herself soaked in his/her own blood. Small wonder then that the vampire was the most horrific and abhorred of scourges and that church and layman alike dealt with the creature drastically whenever and wherever he could be found.

Apart from the stake, the crucifix, fire and daylight, a sexton's spade was often found efficacious in lopping off a vampire's head when discovered in his trance-like sleep. This consecrated weapon is often a favourite device of fiction writers and figures in many modern films on the subject. The stake itself had to be of a particular wood if it was to be effective in its purpose. Aspen wood was held in the Middle Ages to be the best for the task, but hawthorn and maple were also favoured.

The hypnotic power of the vampire was also of great use to the creature in getting at victims who were adequately guarded indoors; the vampire could summon its victim by sheer power of will and this, combined with the baleful hypnotic glow of its eyes, could lure the victim from his household to destruction. Once within its own territory, usually a graveyard, vault or deserted building far from the haunts of man, the vampire would then be free to begin its unholy feasting.

In these cases, unless help were near, things would go ill for the victim. Even if restored to his family he would most likely return to the vampire's terrain of his own volition the following night, as his will power had been drained from him along with his blood. In the open, a vampire has more ease of movement, and even for his potential destroyer, he is a menacing and formidable figure.

As noted, he can change his shape into a bat or wolf; can come and go as mist or vapour; and has lightning-like rapidity of movement. But the vampire-hunter also has many efficacious methods at his disposal. At all times he should wear the crucifix; he can also make a holy circle of herbs or holy water, which the vampire is powerless to cross; and can sometimes trap the vampire within a circle of his own making. For time is on his side. Particularly in summer the vampire has only a few hours for its unholy work and will be destroyed utterly if daylight finds him still abroad.

The vampire-hunter can also throw holy water upon him, in which case the effect will be that of molten lead; the creature will be burnt and scarred and for these and other reasons, the vampire seldom reveals himself to those other than his potential victims. The destroyer of a vampire must also be as cunning as the prey he hunts and the successful practitioners, both in life as well as in fiction, have become justly celebrated.

But what of the vampire's victims, who, dying at last, are laid to " rest "—a rest unknown to the Christian and one in which they walk as soul-less automata and as completely subservient to their unholy master as any Haitian zombie? The church had another answer for this in olden times; anyone suspected of having died of the vampire's kiss was buried with a fragment of the consecrated Host upon their breast. This meant that they could never walk again and in fleshly dissolution found peace.

In various parts of the world vampires are held to be gaunt and of enormous strength; while in places like England and Western Europe they are reputed to be plump, sleek and of an unhealthy pallor. One of the former was the evil manifestation of a history related by the late Dr. Montague Summers in his fascinating *The Vampire; His Kith and· Kin*. Summers speaks of an eighteenth-century infestation in Hungary, where a vampire, which had issued from a nearby cemetery, terrorised a village for three or four years. A Hungarian who visited the place told the locals that he could cope with the evil and lay the vampire to rest.

Summers relates:

In order to fulfil his promise he mounted the clock-tower of the church and watched for the moment when the vampire came out of his grave, leaving behind him in the tomb his shroud and cerements, before he made his way to the village to plague and terrify the in-habitants.

When the Hungarian from his coign of vantage had seen the vampire depart on his prowl, he promptly descended from the tower, possessed himself of the shroud and linen, carrying them off with him back to the belfry. The vampire in due course returned and not finding his cere-cloths ·cried out mightily against the thief who, from the top of the belfry was making signs to him that he should climb and recover his winding-sheet if he wished to get it back again.

The vampire accordingly, began to clamber up the steep stair which led to the summit of the tower, but the Hungarian suddenly gave him such a blow that he fell from top to bottom. Thereupon they were able to strike off his head with the sharp edge of a sexton's spade, and that made an end of the whole business.

The strong-nerved Hungarian was evidently in the mould of Bram Stoker's famous fictional vampire-hunter, Abraham van Helsing, and the tale, laconically recounted by Summers, has all the hair-raising terror of actuality in its bald treatment of detail.

Other traits of the vampire may be briefly dealt with; in Bulgaria a vampire returning from the tomb is supposed to have only one nostril, while in Poland a sharp point at the end of his tongue, like a bee-sting, is held to be the tell-tale sign. In some districts of Europe, even to this day, those with hare-lips are avoided as being of the vampire clan.

Long and crooked fingers and long nails with dirt encrusted under them are other, less evidential pointers, while a pestilential stench as from the charnel house distinguishes their breath. In many countries people with blue eyes are believed to be particularly prone to vampirism, though this theory may be confidently discounted in modern times.

Areas of swamp and marshland, with their unhealthy atmospheres, have long been held to be the abode of the vampire and there is something eerie about such terrain, with thin mist rising slowly from the marshes, which persists even into the latter half of the twentieth century. Gaseous marsh-lights or will-o'-the-wisps which are endemic to swamps have further coloured this legend.

I think I have said enough here to indicate why the legend of the vampire should still have power to arouse horror and terror in an age when electric light and modern accoutrements should have long banished such primal fears. Let us end this chapter with a fine description by Summers of the marsh-vampire, one not, so far as I know, met with elsewhere in the literature on the subject.

In some traditions the vampire is said to float into the house in the form of a mist, a belief which is found in countries so far separate as Hungary and China. In the latter empire wills-o'-the wisp are thought to be an unmistakable sign of a place where much blood has been shed, such as an old battlefield, and all mists and gaseous marsh-lights are connected with the belief in vampires and spectres which convey disease.

Since the effluvia, the vapour and haze from a swamp or quaggy ground are notoriously unhealthy and malarial fevers result in delirium and anaemia, it may be that in some legends the disease has been personified as a ghastly creature who rides on the infected air and sucks the life from his victims.

FOUR

The Vampire of Meduegna

No HISTORY of the vampire in legend would be complete without one of the most famous cases of the eighteenth century, the vampire of Meduegna, near Belgrade. Summers again is the primal source for the tale which appeared in one of his weighty volumes, *The Vampire in Europe*.

According to Summers, this was one of the best-attested and most detailed accounts and a document which gave the facts was signed by three army surgeons and counter-signed by a lieutenant-colonel and a sub-lieutenant on 7th January 1732.

The surgeons were Isaac Siedel, Johannes Flickinger and Johann Baumgartner and according to them the vampiric manifestation concerned a young man named Arnold Paole who returned to his native Meduegna from service in the Levant in the spring of 1727.

He purchased a cottage and 2 acres of land and settled down, which aroused some speculation among the inhabitants, who wondered why such a young man should retire from active life in his early prime.

Though he was honest in his dealings and steady in his conduct the locals were nevertheless worried about a certain strangeness in his manner, though they could never exactly pinpoint their suspicions in any given direction. As time passed he paid court to Nina, the young daughter of a rich farmer whose land ran parallel to his own and later his engagement was announced. But despite their closeness the girl always felt there was a shadow between them and eventually she asked him about the troubles which seemed to oppress him.

Paole told her he was always haunted by fears of an early death, an omen which had begun with a strange adventure which befell him during his Army service at Kostartsa in Greece. He told his fiancée that in those parts the dead returned to torment the living; by an ill chance he had been stationed in a reputedly haunted spot and had experienced a visitation from an undead being. But he had sought out the unhallowed grave and had executed summary vengeance upon the vampire. He had then resigned from the army and literally fled home to his native village.

Summers continues,

It was true that so far he experienced no ill effects and he trusted that he might have been able to counteract the evil. It so happened that during the harvest-home Arnold fell from the top of a loaded hay-waggon and was picked up insensible from the ground. They carried him to bed but he had evidently received some serious injury for after lingering a short time he died. In a few days his body was laid to rest, as they thought, in the village churchyard.

About a month later, however, reports began to be circulated that Arnold had been seen wandering about the village after nightfall and several people whose names are entered upon the official report, complained that they were haunted by him and that after he had appeared to them they felt in a state of extraordinary debility. But a short time went by when several of these persons died and something like a panic began to spread through the neighbourhood.

As the dark winter nights approached no man dared to venture outside his doors when once dusk had fallen, yet it was whispered that the spectre was able easily to penetrate closed windows and walls; that no locks or bars could keep him out if he wished to enter. Throughout the whole winter the wretched village seems to have lived in a state of frantic terror and dismay. The evil, as we may well imagine, was aggravated by the cold hungry nights of a snow-tossed December and January.

At length some ten weeks, or rather more, after his funeral it was resolved that the body of Arnold must be disinterred with a view of ascertaining whether he was indeed a vampire. The party consisted of two officers, military representatives from Belgrade, two Army surgeons, a drummer boy who carried their cases of instruments, the authorities of the village, the old sexton and his assistants.

One of those present describes the scene:

It was early on a grey morning that the commission visited the quiet cemetery of Meduegna which, surrounded with a wall of un-hewn stone, lies sheltered by the mountains that, rising in undulating green slopes, irregularly planted with fruit trees, ends in an abrupt craggy ridge, feathered with underwood. The graves were, for the most part, neatly kept, with borders of box, or something like it, and flowers between; and at the head of most a small wooden cross painted black, bearing the name of the tenant. Here and there a stone had been raised.

One of considerable height, a single narrow slab, ornamented with grotesque Gothic carvings, dominated the rest. Near this lay the grave of Arnold Paole, towards which the party moved. The work of throwing out the earth was begun by the bent, crooked old sexton, who lived in the Leichenhaus beyond the great crucifix. He seemed unconcerned enough.

But as might well be supposed the young drummer boy was gazing intently, fascinated by horror and suspense. Before very long the coffin was rather roughly dragged out of the ground, and the gravedigger's assistant soon knocked off the lid. It was seen that the corpse had moved to one side, the jaws gaped wide open and the blue lips were moist with new blood which had trickled in a thin stream from the corner of the mouth. All unafraid the old sexton caught the body and twisted it straight.

" So ", he cried, " you have not wiped your mouth since last night's work." Even the officers accustomed to the horrors of the battlefield and the surgeons accustomed to the horrors of the dissecting room shuddered at so hideous a spectacle. It is recorded that the drummer boy swooned upon the spot. Nerving themselves to their awful work they inspected the remains more closely and it was soon apparent that there lay before them the thing they dreaded—the vampire. He looked, indeed, as if he had not been dead a day. On handling the corpse the scarfskin came off and below there were new skin and new nails.

Accordingly they scattered garlic over the remains and drove a stake through the body, which it is said, gave a piercing shriek as the warm blood spouted out in a great crimson jet. When this dreadful operation had been performed they proceeded to exhume the bodies of four others who had died in consequence of Arnold's attacks. The records give no details of the state in which these were found. They simply say that whitethorn stakes were driven through them and that they were all five burned. The ashes of all were replaced in consecrated ground.

It might have been thought that these measures would have put an end to vampirism in the village, but such unhappily was not the case, which shows that the original vampire at Kostartsa must have been of an exceptionally malignant nature. About half a dozen years after the body of Arnold Paole had been cremated the infection seems to have broken out afresh and several persons died apparently through loss of blood, their bodies being in a terribly anaemic and attenuated condition. This time the officials did not hesitate immediately to cope with the danger, and they determined to make a complete examination of all the graves in the cemetery to which any suspicion attached.

It was then that the commission of enquiry was set up and the medical reports signed in 1732. The doctors found an extraordinary situation in the ancient cemetery. A 20-year-old woman named Stana, who had died only three months earlier, after a three-day illness, had confessed in dying that she had anointed herself with the blood of a vampire to liberate herself from his persecutions. She and her new-born baby had died, but because of careless interment the child's body had been dug up and devoured by wolves. But the body of the girl was untouched by decay; the chest was full of fresh blood and the viscera, on examination, was in a healthy condition. There was also clean new skin and nails on both hands and feet in this case.

The bodies of a number of women and children were also disinterred and all found to be in a healthy and plump condition, their external appearances as in life and their bodies full of liquid blood. Yet other corpses buried nearby of persons who had died only a short while before were already far gone in decomposition.

Summers concludes his sombre account by saying: " It should be observed that this list by no means exhausts the cases of vampirism which were then collected, and particular details, moreover, have been most fully recorded in each instance, but to amplify the catalogue would involve much reiteration that might prove wearisome without adding anything material to the tale of a demonstration already conclusively established."

FIVE

𝔅ats, 𝔐oths and ℭats

To MOST people the idea of the vampire bat is almost as abhorrent as that of the vampire as a supernatural being. Certainly the bat, with its sinister appearance, pointed fox-like ears and habit of hanging upside down in dark caves must have seemed particularly terrifying to ancient peoples and its emergence at dusk to flit eerily over the countryside would certainly have done much to reinforce the legend.

Yet many bats are perfectly harmless, feeding on fruit, nectar and great numbers of poisonous insects as well as small animals such as mice. Some have a 2-foot wingspan, yet the true vampire bat, which inhabits parts of South America and other tropical countries, is only one among more than 1,200 known species and there are estimated to be billions in existence at any given time. This remarkable mammal, which has many complex qualities not readily apprehended by human beings, plays an important part in the pollination and dispersal of seed on this planet.

The true vampire bat is quite a small beast, though its features are like something out of a nightmare and readily reinforce its fearsome, if somewhat over-rated reputation. Few human beings have been killed by vampire bats; innumerable cattle and other smaller animals provide the greater part of their victims.

The common vampire has two, needle-sharp and quite large teeth set just below its broad and ugly snout; its large eyes are set low down at the side of its muzzle which give it an extraordinary aspect and its lower lip has a great cleft in it which enables it to sink the teeth down into whatever it gets hold of. Like the vampire of legend the wounds it inflicts are superficial and it confines itself to blood alone. The bat has a comparatively long life for such a frail creature and it is surprisingly adaptable.

However, it has many less pleasant characteristics than its gentleness in breaking the skin of its victims. It spreads rabies throughout herds of cattle and horses it attacks in South America. It carries fleas on its fur, like most bats, and is the one known creature which generates rabies without itself falling victim to it.

In a country like Guyana large numbers of animals on the ranges in the savannah areas are lost every year through its activities. It has been estimated that three to four hundred head of cattle and horses on one ranch alone each year will die because of the vampire bat. These ranches, of course, are vast empires of rangeland by comparison to European standards, with thousands of head of cattle, but even so the depredations of the vampire bat are alarming.

It drinks the blood of animals and birds by sinking its short incisor teeth in the upper jaw into its victims, usually on the back or the neck, while they are totally unaware that their blood is being drunk. In Guyana the vampire bat is quite a small mammal, not much larger than a man's two hands with its wings spread, contrary to popular superstition. It usually lives in caves or under the hollows of cliffs. It drains 2 ounces of blood each night in order to live and in all is known to drink 6 to 7 gallons of blood a year.

There are, in fact, only two species of blood-sucking bats known, the *Diphylla ecaudata* and the *Desmodus rufus*, both of which are restricted to Central and South America. Their depredations among cattle and their occasional attacks on human beings were noted by early writers on exploration and in the eighteenth century their activities were such as to destroy whole herds introduced by the missionaries. They were also noted to have attacked domestic fowl, drawing blood from the birds' combs until they turned white from anaemia.

For many years, until it was established otherwise, early naturalists claimed that the huge bat *Vampyrus spectrum*, was a vampire, but in fact it turned out to be frugivorous. The wounds the vampire inflicts are very much like a small cut from a sharp razor, such as would be made by a man while shaving. When the skin is

(*left*) Raymond Huntley, who, at the age of 22, created the role of Dracula on the English stage. (*right*) Bela Lugosi, the first Dracula on the American stage and on the screen

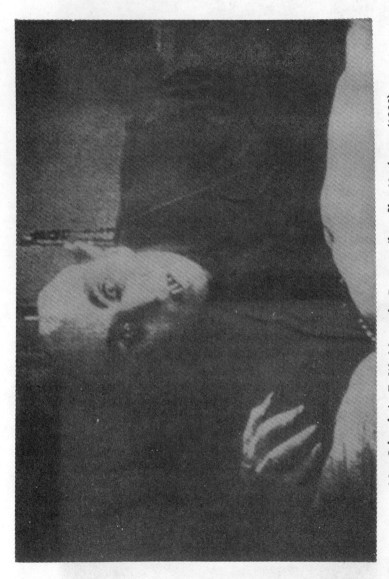

Max Schreck in F. W. Murnau's German silent film *Nosferatu* (1922)

taken off a number of capillary vessels are exposed and a constant blood-flow ensured.

The blood is then drawn through the bat's small gullet into its intestine-like stomach, where it is slowly digested while the mammal hangs upside down from a tree or roof of a cave. Though the vampire has been known to draw blood from the necks of sleeping natives it largely has an undeserved reputation as a killer of men.

As recently as 1969 a new horror was revealed to the world by a Swiss entomologist, Dr. Hans Banziger, who discovered a vampire moth while working in Malaya. In that year he published the first observations on the blood-sucking moth which pierces the skin to extract the life-giving fluid. Dr. Banziger, in his findings, given to science in the Bulletin of Entomological Research, said that the nocturnal moth, *Calyptra eustrigata*, had evolved a proboscis tough enough to penetrate mammalian skin.

Other members of the Calyptra family feed on the juice of ripe fruit, which they pierce with the proboscis, but the *eustrigata* has apparently taken the process one stage further and evolved as the first member of the moth family to become a true vampire.

The insect's proboscis has a hard, sharp point, and in the hills near Kuala Lumpur Dr. Banziger has observed the moth going about its business. It attacks a wide variety of animals, ranging from antelope to buffalo and deer and has been seen feeding on animal blood for periods of as long as an hour at a time. Human subjects have taken part in laboratory tests; the two halves of the proboscis act like saws, moving alternately to make their cuts and penetrate about 5 millimetres beneath the skin to become effective.

Those taking part in the experiments in the laboratory told the doctor that the moth's action felt like " being stabbed with a red-hot needle ". On occasion the blood extracted has been regurgitated and Dr. Banziger believes the moth may be a potential carrier of disease. So far as is known the moth does not attack human beings in the field, but the future possibility cannot be ruled out.

Returning to the field of legend, the French scholar Dr. Fernand Mery in his fascinating study, *The Cat*, first published in France in 1966, mentions the folk-tale of the Vampire Cat of Nabeshima in medieval Japan. A frightening engraving of the period shows the cat, a mottled black and grey, attacking a

holder and sinking its teeth into his throat in the
er of the vampire in human form.

is unusual because in Asian folklore most cats are
evolent and tales of evil cats are rare. Cats in human
ever, abound in Eastern folklore, very often in the form
wives who slip out at night to their lovers in the shape
of innocent animals and return the same way at dawn, while their
husbands are still sleeping.

More germane to the legend of the vampire is the extraordinary
engraving by the German artist Kirchner who, in a work of 1667
depicts a gigantic cat in the form of a bat. The creature, which
has the head of a tabby, is hovering against a wall with its bat-
wings outspread, apparently about to swoop on a group of three
mice in the foreground. Another curious feature of this engraving
is the fact that the cat has the breasts of a woman. What the
artist meant by it is not known, but the cat had an evil reputation
in many parts of the world, particularly in ancient times. Certainly the vampire cat has its own small, but secure place, in the
dark story of the vampire.

SIX

𝕬𝖚𝖌𝖚𝖘𝖙𝖚𝖘 𝕳𝖆𝖗𝖊'𝖘 𝖁𝖆𝖒𝖕𝖎𝖗𝖊

WE RETURN to the nineteenth century for one of the most vivid and exciting manifestations of vampirism, that related by Augustus Hare and generally referred to under the title of Croglin Low Hall. Though many writers have taken this piece of high romanticism as factual, I think I am justified in placing it among the legendary manifestations.

Hare; a celebrated Victorian diarist and man-about-town was notoriously vague as to detail in some of the taller stories in his journals and jottings, but his tale is none the worse for that. It appeared in *The Story of My Life*, published many years ago and bears all the hall-marks of the romantic fiction of the period.

It was purportedly narrated to Hare by a certain Captain Fisher. Hare continues:

" Fisher," said the Captain, " may sound a very plebeian name, but this family is of a very ancient lineage, and for many hundreds of years they have possessed a very curious old place in Cumberland, which bears the weird name of Croglin Grange. The great characteristic of the house is that never at any period of its very long existence has it been more than one storey high, but it has a terrace from which large grounds sweep away towards the church in the hollow, and a fine distant view.

When, in lapse of years, the Fishers outgrew Croglin Grange in family and fortune, they were wise enough not to destroy the long-standing characteristic of the place by adding another storey to the house, but they went away to the south, to reside at Thorncombe near Guildford, and they let Croglin Grange.

They were extremely fortunate in their tenants, two brothers and a sister. They heard their praises from all quarters. To their poorer neighbours they were all that is most kind and beneficent, and their neighbours of a higher class spoke of them as a most welcome addition to the little society of the neighbourhood. On their part, the tenants were greatly delighted with their new residence. The arrangement of the house, which would have been a trial to many, was not so to them. In every respect Croglin Grange was exactly suited to them.

The winter was spent most happily by the new inmates of Croglin Grange, who shared in all the little social pleasures of the district, and made themselves very popular. In the following summer there was one day which was dreadfully, annihilatingly hot. The brothers lay under the trees with their books, for it was too hot for any active occupation. The sister sat in the veranda and worked, or tried to work, for in the intense sultriness of that summer day, work was next to impossible. They dined early, and after dinner they still sat out on the veranda, enjoying the cool air which came with the evening, and they watched the sun set, and the moon rise over the belt of trees which separated the grounds from the church yard, seeing it mount the heavens till the whole lawn was bathed in silver light, across which the long shadows from the shrubbery fell as if embossed, so vivid and distinct were they.

When they separated for the night, all retiring to their rooms on the ground floor (for, as I said, there was no upstairs in that house), the sister felt that the heat was still so great that she could not sleep, and having fastened her window, she did not close the shutters—in that very quiet place it was not necessary—and, propped against the pillows, she still watched the wonderful, the marvellous beauty of that summer night. Gradually she became aware of two lights, two lights which flickered in and out in the belt of trees which separated the lawn from the church yard, and, as her gaze became fixed upon them, she saw them emerge, fixed in a dark substance, a definite ghastly something, which seemed every moment to become nearer, increasing in size and substance as it approached. Every now and then it was lost for a moment in the long shadows which stretched across the lawn from the trees, and then it emerged larger than ever, and still coming on. As she watched it, the most uncontrollable horror seized her. She longed to get away, but the door was close to the window, and the door was locked on the inside, and while she was unlocking it she must be for an instant nearer to it. She longed to scream, but her voice seemed paralysed, her tongue glued to the roof of her mouth. Suddenly—she could never explain why afterwards—the terrible object seemed to turn to one side, seemed to be going round the house, not to þe coming to her at all, and immediately she jumped out of bed and rushed to the door, but as she was unlocking it she heard scratch, scratch, scratch upon the window, and saw a hideous brown face with flaming eyes glaring in at her. She rushed back to the bed, but the creature continued to scratch, scratch, scratch upon the window. She felt a sort of mental comfort in the knowledge that the window was securely fastened on the inside. Suddenly the scratching sound ceased, and a kind of pecking sound took its place. Then, in her agony, she became aware that the creature was unpicking the lead! The noise continued, and a diamond pane of glass fell into the room. Then a long bony finger of the creature came in and turned the handle of the window, and the window opened, and the creature came in; and it came across the room, and her terror was so great that she could not scream, and it came up to the bed, and it twisted its long, bony fingers into her hair, and it dragged her head over the side of the bed, and—it bit her violently in the throat.

As it bit her, her voice was released, and she screamed with all her might and main. Her brothers rushed out of their rooms, but the door was locked on the inside. A moment was lost while they got a poker and broke it open. Then the creature had already escaped through the window, and the sister, bleeding violently from a wound in the throat, was lying unconscious over the side of the bed. One brother pursued the creature, which fled before him through the moonlight with gigantic strides, and eventually seemed to disappear over the wall into the churchyard. Then he rejoined his brother by the sister's bedside. She was dreadfully hurt, and her wound was a very definite one, but she was of strong disposition, not even given to romance or superstition, and when she came to herself she said, ' What has happened is most extraordinary and I am very much hurt. It seems inexplicable, but of course there is an explanation, and we must wait for it. It will turn out that a lunatic has escaped from some asylum and found his way here.' The wound healed, and she appeared to get well, but the doctor who was sent for to her would not believe that she could bear so terrible a shock so easily, and insisted that she must have change, mental and physical; so her brothers took her to Switzerland.

Being a sensible girl, when she went abroad she threw herself at once into the interests of the country she was in. She dried plants, she made sketches, she went up mountains, and, as autumn came on, she was the person who urged that they should return to

Croglin Grange. 'We have taken it,' she said, 'for seven years, and we have only been there one; and we shall always find it difficult to let a house which is only one storey high, so we had better return there; lunatics do not escape every day.' As she urged it, her brothers wished nothing better, and the family returned to Cumberland. From there being no upstairs in the house it was impossible to make any great change in their arrangements. The sister occupied the same room, but it is unnecessary to say she always closed the shutters, which, however, as in many old houses, always left one top pane of the window uncovered. The brothers moved, and occupied a room together, exactly opposite that of their sister, and they always kept loaded pistols in their room.

The winter passed most peacefully and happily. In the following March, the sister was suddenly awakened by a sound she remembered only too well—scratch, scratch, scratch upon the window, and, looking up, she saw, climbed up to the topmost pane of the window, the same hideous brown shrivelled face, with glaring eyes, looking in at her. This time she screamed as loud as she could. Her brothers rushed out of their room with pistols, and out of the front door. The creature was already scudding away across the lawn. One of the brothers fired and hit it in the leg, but still with the other leg it continued to make way, scrambled over the wall into the churchyard, and seemed to disappear into a vault which belonged to a family long extinct.

The next day the brothers summoned all the tenants of Croglin Grange, and in their presence the vault was opened. A horrible scene revealed itself. The vault was full of coffins; they had been broken open, and their contents, horribly mangled and distorted, were scattered over the floor. One coffin alone remained intact. Of that the lid had been lifted, but still lay loose upon the coffin. They raised it, and there, brown, withered, shrivelled, mummified, but quite entire, was the same hideous figure which had looked in at the windows of Croglin Grange, with the marks of a recent pistol-shot in the leg: and they did the only thing that can lay a vampire —they burnt it."

On this high note we turn from the vampire of legend and follow the grim adventures of the monster as manifested through its earliest appearances in fiction down to present times.

In Literature

SEVEN

𝔓𝔬𝔩𝔦𝔡𝔬𝔯𝔦 𝔖𝔢𝔱𝔰 𝔞 𝔗𝔯𝔢𝔫𝔡

THE VAMPIRE entered into literature as a fictional character for the first time with the advent of John Polidori. The birth of the genre was long overdue and it is surprising that it was not until early in the nineteenth century that this horrific theme was made the subject of a full-scale novel, though the vampire was not unknown to poetry with such works as *Lenore* by Burger, which had appeared nearly three decades earlier, and Goethe had also made some use of it.

But it was left to Polidori, a friend of Byron and his personal physician, to create literary history with a fiendish portrait of a ruthless vampiric character, which sent a ripple of excitement through the cultivated and literary-minded of Europe. Though the least talented of them, Polidori formed the fourth of a quartet in whose company he would have shone had not the other three been artists of genius. They were of course, Byron himself and his two friends, the poet Percy Bysshe Shelley and his wife, the novelist Mary Wollstonecraft.

The occasion which gave birth to one of the great literary horror stories and the first masterpiece of the genre, Mary Shelley's *Frankenstein*, is well-known. Byron and his companions were fond of telling each other ghost stories on long winter evenings on the Continent and it was assumed for many years that Polidori's tale had been written by Byron. He called it, not surprisingly, *The Vampyre*, and though it swept Europe and went into many different editions, it has been out of print for many years and is largely forgotten today except by scholars and those with a taste for literary curiosities.

Mary Shelley's great classic was first published in 1818 and the name of Lord Ruthven was introduced to a fascinated public for the first time in the following year. Surprisingly, Mary Shelley took only a few months to write *Frankenstein*, which had been first suggested to her by the conversation of the four friends in January or February of 1818, when presumably Polidori received the inspiration for his own tale. *Frankenstein* was already in print by the autumn but it was not until more than a year later that the first literary vampire was walking the night and sending delicious shudders down the comfortable spines of readers sated with port and good food.

The eighteenth and nineteenth centuries were, of course, the great ages for both writers and readers, the former having the time and patience to weave their massive novels; the readers—or at least the well-to-do and cultivated, who made up the greater part of the literate classes at that time—having the leisure and the long winter evenings to plough their way through the weighty three-volume novels of the era. The atmosphere of the age itself was conducive to both the writing and reading of such fiction and the public found *The Vampyre* greatly to its taste. A trend was set which has continued into the late twentieth century and shows no sign of abating.

Polidori suffered initially, as do many men who live in a greater shadow, of having his own work passed off as that of a genius, for it was assumed by many that *The Vampyre* was the creation of Byron himself. It passed through a number of editions as being from his pen and it was not until some years later that Dr. Polidori was given full credit for his demoniac invention; some earlier editions, as was the custom in those days, had appeared anonymously.

Lord Ruthven, in Polidori's immensely long and involved fantasy, set the pattern for all such vampire-heroes in literature and was not to be toppled from his throne until the advent of Count Dracula almost eighty years later.

The Vampyre first appeared in *The New Monthly Magazine* of 1st April 1819, when it was announced as being "A Tale by Lord Byron". Such was its content that despite its great length and somewhat melodramatic style—which was exaggerated even for its day—it created an immediate sensation. It ran to many editions and as well as being admired was also imitated on the Continent of Europe.

Polidori's story begins with a long preamble which details something of the legends of the vampire and an editorial note says, " These human blood-suckers fattened—and their veins became distended to such a state of repletion as to cause the blood to flow from all the passages of their bodies and even from the very pores of their skins ". It says much for the tenacity of the reader of the time that he followed the editor who continues for several pages, quoting poems and copious notes until Polidori's novel is encrusted with a barnacle-like apparatus of editorial sermonising.

But once Polidori's pen is allowed to begin his tale the story, which runs to several hundred pages, is such as to have fascinated his contemporaries, though it makes fairly heavy going for the modern reader.

The satanic Lord Ruthven is introduced at the height of the London season and, like Maturin's great Gothic hero " Melmoth the Wanderer ", gazes around him with melancholy and sombre gaze as though he cannot take part in the revelries of ordinary men. He causes fear and awe among many of those with whom chance brings him into contact. In a striking passage Polidori refers to " the dead grey eye which, fixing upon the object's face, did not seem to penetrate and at one glance to pierce through to the inward working of the heart; but fell upon the cheek with a leaden ray that weighed upon the skin it could not pass ".

Despite this he befriends a young man called Aubrey who joins the nobleman in a trip to the Continent. On their travels young Aubrey has ample opportunity to study his companion and observes that he distributes largesse to worthless people like profligates and gamblers but gives nothing to the really deserving. But, surprisingly, those in receipt of his charity find a curse on it and either end on the scaffold or in abject poverty.

In Rome Aubrey frustrates Ruthven's designs in attempting to ruin a young girl and in a letter from his guardian learns that since Lord Ruthven left London all sorts of iniquities and awful scandals concerning his noble companion have come to light. He parts from Ruthven and eventually finds himself in Athens. Here, there are long literary diversions much loved by authors of Polidori's vintage, which however, need not bother us here.

Aubrey falls in love with a young Greek girl, Ianthe, and

pursues his antiquarian studies. In a scene which was to become the pattern for such literary exercises he proposes to visit a certain site but is warned by Ianthe's parents that the place is a resort of vampires. Like all such heroes since, Aubrey laughs at this notion and in a well-observed scene is overtaken by darkness and a heavy storm many miles from home.

In a sequence more reminiscent of the wilder shores of operatic licence but one more familiar within the tenets of the Gothic novel, Aubrey's horse deposits him before a hut in a forest. He hears a girl scream, bursts through the door and after a terrific fight in the darkened hut with a being of tremendous strength is dashed to the ground. Subsequently, he is found by peasants lying half senseless; worse is to follow, however. Nearby lies the body of Ianthe, with the marks of the vampire on her throat. Aubrey falls ill with a raging fever and the heart-broken parents die of grief! One can almost see the curtain coming down for the first interval.

But Polidori has more shrewd plot-points for the contemporary reader; Lord Ruthven arrives in Athens and nurses Aubrey with such tenderness and diligence that all the young hero's suspicions are forgotten. Later, in a remote part of Greece the pair are attacked by brigands and Ruthven receives a mortal wound. Dying, he extracts a promise from Aubrey that he will not tell anyone of his death " for a year and a day ". Aubrey agrees and when Ruthven dies has the body transported to a lonely mountain peak but it later disappears. As might be imagined, Aubrey is sorely puzzled by all these mysterious happenings, particularly by the sight of an ornamental sheath among Ruthven's effects, which exactly fits the dagger found near the hut where Ianthe died.

Already Polidori has used up as many pages as most modern writers would use for a complete novel but he is hardly begun; to thread all through the convoluted plot would be wearisome but Polidori's ingenuity must be admired and, of course, like Dickens, his methods were admirably suited to periodical publication, when the reader would be kept waiting for a week or a month to see what happened next.

After many adventures Aubrey returns to London, where he is due to present his sister into society. The contemporary reader's horror may be imagined when, in another striking scene, Polidori has a familiar voice mutter in Aubrey's ear, " Remember your oath ". Turning, he finds the figure of the dead Lord Ruthven standing near him at a gay drawing-room party. He sees the figure again a few nights later and like Macbeth, haunted by a phantom no one else apparently sees, becomes distracted and in his turn invites comment and almost terror wherever he goes. These scenes are among the best in this long and ingenious book and well justify its reputation at the time it appeared.

Aubrey is consoled by the thought that he will be able to speak when the year and a day is up, but his terrors return tenfold when Polidori carefully prepares his next convolution. The hero's sister, Miss Aubrey, announces her engagement to marry and the young man is delighted until the girl hands him a miniature of her fiancé. He recognises Ruthven in the portrait and in a rage tramples it under foot.

He asks for the marriage to be postponed for twenty-four hours, when the terms of his promise will have expired; but the request is disregarded and in a series of scenes which would now be seen by modern script-writers as " cross-cutting ", Polidori harrows his reader with descriptions of wedding preparations going forward, while Aubrey falls into such rage and depression that a physician orders him to be kept under restraint!

During the night Aubrey discovers that Ruthven had insinuated himself into his sister's affections by visiting the house during his absence and inquiring after his friend's supposed derangement. Where Polidori restrains himself from one of the fatal weaknesses of the Gothic novella of his time, is in the finale of his horrific tale which has all the apparatus of Grand Guignol and no last-minute unexpected—or happy—ending. The unfortunate Aubrey makes his way into the wedding chapel but is seen by Ruthven, who holds him to his promise. Seized by attendants he bursts a blood vessel in his agony of spirit and is taken to bed seriously ill. The accident is kept from the sister, who marries the vampire-nobleman and leaves London with her husband.

Part of Polidori's sombre ending reads, " Aubrey's weakness increased; the effusion of blood produced symptoms of the near approach of death. He desired his sister's guardians might be called and when the midnight hour had struck, he related composedly what the reader has perused—he died immediately after.

" The guardians hastened to protect Miss Aubrey; but when they arrived it was too late. Lord Ruthven had disappeared, and Aubrey's sister had glutted the thirst of a VAMPYRE! "

This surprisingly laconic conclusion had a tremendous effect and Polidori's tale was a deserved sensation; it first appeared in book form in 1819, being published by the firm of Sherwood and rapidly went into many different editions. It was translated into French and published in Paris the same year, 1819 and in addition to German and other different language editions, a number of " sequels " by other hands appeared.

The pattern for other vampire novels was also set with this unique first tale by Polidori; the piece was dramatised by the French playwright Charles Nodier, with collaborators and presented in Paris at the Theatre de la Porte Saint-Martin, still noted in 1973 for the liveliness of its presentations. It had its premiere at this theatre in June 1820 with M. Philippe as Lord Ruthven and had, according to accounts of the time, a quite extraordinary success.

It was also published in France as a piece of theatre and the resulting publicity was so great that the " Saint-Martin " was nightly packed to capacity. The notion of the vampire monster as the hero of a stage-play was vivid and new and the audiences evidently appreciated this, possibly as much for the sexual undertones of the situation, as for the necrophilic implications of the story. The play was revived at the same theatre and with largely the same cast in 1823 and again played to capacity houses.

The great Alexandre Dumas himself was present one evening on this second occasion and recorded his thrills and delight at the situations depicted on the stage. He recalled the evening in his *Memoires*, written many years later. In fact, so impressed was the great novelist-playwright that almost thirty years after, with his long-time collaborator Auguste Maquet he wrote his own drama *Le Vampire* which was presented at the Theatre Ambigu-Comique in December 1851. This had many striking scenes and proved the popularity of the relatively new theme, as it found great favour with its audiences.

As usually happens, between Nodier's piece and that of Dumas, dozens of imitators arose in the theatre in France and elsewhere until the vampire pieces reached ludicrous proportions. Some were even farces with music, which shows how far the imitators had strayed from Polidori's original intention. An operatic version of the Nodier adaptation was produced at the English Opera House, London, in 1820, with T. P. Cooke in the title role, and was a great success also. It was not until 1852 that Polidori's story, dramatised by Dion Boucicault was presented in London. It was later revived as *The Phantom* and also played in New York with some success.

Polidori had struck a chord of horror in the sensibilities of many people in widely differing countries and had secured for himself a small but permanent niche in the history of the vampire as a literary creation. It remained for the amazing and prolific Thomas Preskett Prest to carry the theme a stage further.

EIGHT

Prest's Varney

IT WAS almost thirty years before the vampire was to re-emerge as a major force in popular literature. The credit for this must go to one of the most mysterious and prolific authors and pamphleteers of the nineteenth century, Thomas Preskett Prest. Though he wrote literally dozens of novels of stupefying length—500 to 800 pages was an average stint and 1,000-plus not unusual—only one need concern us here.

Varney the Vampire has a unique place in the genre as it came three decades after *The Vampyre* and slightly less than fifty years before *Dracula*, thus keeping the vampire as a fictional character almost continually before the public during the last century. *Varney*, which was issued in gaudy and lurid covers with drawings that cunningly combined horror and sexuality in one, was one of Prest's more modest works, running only to 868 pages.

Aptly sub-titled, " The Feast of Blood ", *Varney* was a well-contrived and extremely exciting piece of fiction and its 220 chapters gave the public of its day remarkably good value for money. I once discussed this novel with an old friend Peter Haining, a well-known editor in the macabre field, and at the time occupying an important position in one of England's leading paperback publishing houses. For some while I had been trying to obtain copies of such macabre works as *The Monk* and *Varney* and wondered why no modern paperback house would issue them.

Peter explained that with a specialised readership, modern re-issues of such tremendously lengthy works would be prohibitively costly even providing one could run a copy to earth. In fact *Varney the Vampire* is extremely rare nowadays and believed not to exist outside museum libraries and bibliophiles' collections.

Varney was one of Prest's earliest works and was first published in England in 1847. Its horrifying content was to make it a tremendous success, so much so that it was not long before reprints were demanded. In 1853 *Varney* appeared in penny parts from the press of a famous publisher of " penny dreadfuls " of the period, E. Lloyd of Salisbury Square, Fleet Street.

Prest was one of the most successful practitioners of what was later to become the shilling shocker and his powerful imagination and breakneck pace of narrative were epitomised in such racy works as *The Secret of the Grey Turret, The Goblet of Gore, The Skeleton Clutch* and *Sawney Bean.* All these and many others were written and published within a comparatively short span of years and it is interesting to speculate what a man of Prest's capacity for labour could have achieved in modern times with the aid of electric typewriters and the tape recorder.

In these days of mass circulation paperbacks and newspapers Prest's achievement is still impressive and *Varney,* as well as being a keywork in the history of vampire literature, is a prime example of this author's style and method. Prest's name has been kept alive, of course, by his perennially fresh drama of *Sweeney Todd, the Demon Barber of Fleet Street,* versions of which in various media are still current, notably through film and television. *Varney* would make an admirable subject for a horror film and it is surprising that no one has yet adapted it for the screen. The narrative is set in about 1735 and Prest himself hinted that the story was based on real life incidents.

Polidori, Prest and Stoker can truly be said to have created vampire literature and though they did not live to see the phenomenal success of the genre they had fathered, they would doubtless have been astonished at the continuing popularity of the theme.

It is a rather strange fact that the werewolf, with which vampirism shares many traits—e.g. the efficacy of silver bullets and the transformation into a wolf—has not been nearly such a popular theme in fiction, even though it is every bit as imaginative and exciting. Guy Endore fathered the nearest thing to a classic in the extremely well-written and constructed, *The Werewolf of Paris,* and apart from Sheridan le Fanu and a handful of other writers in modern times, including myself, the theme has been but sparingly evoked in the short story field.

As already noted, the sexual theme in vampirism may have had a lot to do with it; that there is a strong element of sexualism there can be little doubt. Like beauty and the beast it has undeniable sexual overtones and both in literature and the cinema, the heroine is usually a young and beautiful girl who is attacked by a male vampire who, while horrific and deadly, is at least usually handsome in a cruel way.

There is a good reason for this if the author is to succeed in his intention of making the theme palatable to his reader; the vampire of legend, if not of fact, would have been extremely repellent, both physically and otherwise and it is not surprising that fiction writers preferred to turn to something a little more prepossessing in depicting their villains.

Prest's *Varney* combined repellent qualities with animal magnetism and, as has been mentioned, there was a strong sexual element, both in the choice of victim and in the illustrations accompanying the text. Prest scored too on the amount of research and scholarship he put into *Varney* and there is no doubt that he had learned a great deal about his subject, from the unusual and detailed touches he introduced no less than in the grand flourishes of his big scenes. His opening chapter could hardly be bettered, even in the florid school of literature at which he excelled. He captions it, in typical period style, " Midnight—The Hail Storm—The Dreadful Visitor. The Vampyre "

The solemn tones of the old cathedral clock have announced midnight—the air is thick and heavy—a strange, death-like stillness pervades all nature. Like the ominous calm which precedes some more than usually terrific outbreak of the elements, they seem to have paused even in their ordinary fluctuations, to gather a terrific strength for the great effort. A faint peal of thunder now comes from far off. Like a signal gun for the battle of the winds to begin, it appeared to awaken them from their lethargy, and one awful, warring hurricane swept over a whole city, producing more devastation in the four or five minutes it lasted, than would a half century of ordinary phenomena.

It was as if some giant had blown upon some toy town, and scattered many of the buildings before the hot blast of his terrific breath; for as suddenly as that blast of wind had come did it cease, and all was as still and calm as before.

Sleepers awakened, and thought what they had heard must be the confused chimera of a dream. They trembled and turned to sleep again.

All is still—still as the very grave. Not a sound breaks the magic of repose. What is that—a strange pattering noise, as of a million of fairy feet? It is hail—yes, a hail-storm has burst over the city. Leaves are dashed from the trees, mingled with small boughs; windows that lie most opposed to the direct fury of the pelting particles of ice are broken, and the rapt repose that before was so remarkable in its intensity, is exchanged for a noise which, in its accumulation, drowns every cry of surprise or consternation which here and there arose from persons who found their houses invaded by the storm.

Now and then, too, there would come a sudden gust of wind that in its strength, as it blew laterally, would, for a moment, hold millions of the hailstones suspended in mid air, but it was only to dash them with redoubled force in some new direction, where more mischief was to be done.

Oh, how the storm raged! Hail—rain—wind. It was, in very truth, an awful night.

There is an antique chamber in an ancient house. Curious and quaint carvings adorn the walls, and the large chimney-piece is a curiosity of itself. The ceiling is low, and a large bay window, from roof to floor, looks to the west. The window is latticed, and filled with curiously painted glass and rich stained pieces, which send in a strange, yet beautiful light, when sun or moon shines into the apartment. There is but one portrait in that room, although the walls seem panelled for the express purpose of containing a series of pictures. The portrait is that of a young man, with a pale face, a stately brow, and a strange expression about the eyes, which no one cared to look on twice.

There is a stately bed in that chamber, of carved walnut-wood is it made, rich in design and elaborate in execution; one of those works of art which owe their existence to the Elizabethan era. It is hung with heavy silken and damask furnishing; nodding feathers are at its corners—covered with dust are they, and they lend a funereal aspect to the room. The floor is of polished oak.

God! how the hail dashes on the old bay window! Like an occasional discharge of mimic musketry, it comes dashing, beating and cracking upon the small panes; but they resist it—their small size saves them: the wind, the hail, the rain, expend their fury in vain.

The bed in that old chamber is occupied. A creature formed in all fashions of loveliness lies in a half sleep upon that ancient couch—a girl young and beautiful as a spring morning. Her long hair has escaped from its confinement and streams over the blackened coverings of the bedstead; she has been restless in her sleep for the clothing of the bed is in much confusion. One arm is over her head, the other hangs nearly off the side of the bed near to which she lies. A neck and bosom that would have formed a study for the rarest sculptor that ever Providence gave genius to, were half disclosed. She moaned slightly in her sleep, and once or twice the lips moved as if in prayer—at least one might judge so, for the name of Him who suffered for all came once faintly from them.

She has endured much fatigue, and the storm does not awaken her; but it can disturb the slumbers it does not possess the power to destroy entirely. The turmoil of the elements wakes the senses, although it cannot entirely break the repose they have lapsed into.

Oh, what a world of witchery was in that mouth, slightly parted, and exhibiting within the pearly teeth that glistened even in the faint light that came from that bay window. How sweetly the long silken eyelashes lay upon the cheek. Now she moves, and one shoulder is entirely visible—whiter, fairer than the spotless clothing of the bed on which she lies, is the smooth skin of that fair creature, just budding into womanhood, and in that transition state which present to us all the charms of the girl—almost of the child, with the more matured beauty and gentleness of advancing years.

Was that lightning? Yes—an awful vivid, terrifying flash—then a roaring peal of thunder, as if a thousand mountains were rolling one over the other in the blue vault of Heaven! Who sleeps now in that ancient city? Not one living soul. The dread trumpet of eternity could not more effectually have awakened any one.

The hail continues. The wind continues. The uproar of the elements seems at its height. Now she awakens—that beautiful girl on the antique bed; she opens those eyes of celestial blue, and a faint cry of alarm bursts from her lips. At least it is a cry which, amid the noise and turmoil without, sounds but faint and weak. She sits upon the bed and presses her hands upon her eyes. Heavens! what a wild torrent of wind and rain, and hail! The thunder likewise seems intent upon awakening sufficient echoes to last until the next flash of forked lightning should again produce the wild concussion of the air. She murmurs a prayer—a prayer for those she loves best; the names of those dear to her gentle heart come from her lips; she weeps and prays; she thinks then of what devastation the storm must surely produce, and to the great God of Heaven she prays for all living things. Another flash, a wild, blue, bewildering flash of lightning streams across that bay window, for an instant bringing out every colour in it with terrible distinctness. A shriek bursts from the lips of the young girl, and then with eyes fixed upon that window, which, in another moment, is all darkness, and with such an expression of terror upon her face as it had never before known, she trembled, and the perspiration of intense fear stood upon her brow.

"What—what was it?" she gasped; "real, or a delusion? Oh, God, what was it? A figure tall and gaunt, endeavouring from the outside to unclasp the window. I saw it. That flash of lightning revealed it to me. It stood the whole length of the window."

There was a lull of wind. The hail was not falling so thickly—moreover, it now fell, what there was of it, straight, and yet a strange clattering sound came upon the glass of that long window. It could not be a delusion—she is awake, and she hears it. What can produce it? Another flash of lightning—another shriek—there could be now no delusion.

A tall figure is standing on the ledge immediately outside the window. It is its finger-nails upon the glass that produce the sound so like the hail, now that the hail has ceased. Intense fear paralysed the limbs of that beautiful girl. That one shriek is all she can utter—with hands clasped, a face of marble, a heart beating so wildly in her bosom, that each moment it seems as if it would break its confines, eyes distended and fixed upon the window, she waits, froze with horror. The pattering and clattering of the nails continues. No word is spoken, and now she fancies she can trace the darker form of that figure against the window, and she can see the long arms moving to and fro, feeling for some mode of entrance. What strange light is that which now gradually creeps up into the air? red and terrible—brighter and brighter it grows. The lightning has set fire to a mill, and the reflection of the rapidly consuming building falls upon that long window. There can be no mistake. The figure is there, still feeling for an entrance, and clattering against the glass with its long nails, that appear as if the growth of many years had been untouched. She tries to scream again but a choking sensation comes over her, and she cannot. It is too dreadful—she tries to move—each limb seems wedged down by tons of lead—she can but in a hoarse faint whisper cry—

"Help—help—help—help!"

And that one word she repeats like a person in a dream. The red glare of the fire continues. It throws up the tall gaunt figure in hideous relief against the long window. It shows, too, upon the one portrait that is in the chamber, and that portrait appears to fix its eyes upon the attempting intruder, while the flickering light from the fire makes it look fearfully lifelike. A small pane of glass is broken, and the form without introduces a long gaunt hand, which seems utterly destitute of flesh. The fastening is removed, and one half of the window, which opens like folding doors, is swung wide open upon its hinges.

And yet now she could not scream—she could not move. " Help —help!—help!—" was all she could say. But, oh, that look of terror that sat upon her face, it was dreadful—a look to haunt the memory for a life-time—a look to obtrude itself upon the happiest moments, and turn them to bitterness.

The figure turns half round, and the light falls upon the face. It is perfectly white—perfectly bloodless. The eyes look like polished tin; the lips are drawn back, and the principal feature next to those dreadful eyes is the teeth—the fearful looking teeth—projecting like those of some wild animal, hideously, glaringly white, and fang-like. It approaches the bed with a strange, gliding movement. It clashes together the long nails that literally appear to hang from the finger ends. No sound comes from its lips. Is she going mad?— that young and beautiful girl exposed to so much terror; she has drawn up all her limbs; she cannot even now say help. The power of articulation is gone, but the power of movement has returned to her; she can draw herself slowly along to the other side of the bed from that towards which the hideous appearance is coming.

But her eyes are fascinated. The glance of a serpent could not have produced a greater effect upon her than did the fixed gaze of those awful, metallic-looking eyes that were bent on her face. Crouching down so that gigantic height were lost and the horrible, protruding, white face was the most prominent object, came on the figure. What was it?—what did it want there?—what made it look so hideous—so unlike an inhabitant of the earth, and yet to be on it?

Now she has got to the verge of the bed, and the figure pauses. It seemed as if when it paused she lost the power to proceed. The clothing of the bed was now clutched in her hands with unconscious power. She drew her breath short and thick. Her bosom heaves, and her limbs tremble, yet she cannot withdraw her eyes from that marble-looking face. He holds hers with his glittering eye.

The storm has ceased—all is still. The winds are hushed; the church clock proclaims the hour of one: a hissing sound comes from the throat of the hideous being, and he raises his long, gaunt arms—the lips move. He advances. The girl places one small foot from the bed on to the floor. She is unconsciously dragging the clothing with her. The door of the room is in that direction—can she reach it? Has she power to walk?—can she withdraw her eyes from the face of the intruder, and so break the hideous charm? God of Heaven! is it real, or some dream so like reality as to nearly overturn the judgement for ever?

The figure has paused again, and half on the bed and half out of it that young girl lies trembling. Her long hair streams across the entire width of the bed. As she has slowly moved along she has left it streaming across the pillows. The pause lasted about a minute—oh, what an age of agony. That minute was, indeed, enough for madness to do its full work in.

With a sudden rush that could not be foreseen—with a strange howling cry that was enough to awaken terror in every breast, the figure seized the long tresses of her hair, and twining them round his bony hands he held her to the bed. Then she screamed—Heaven granted her that power to scream. Shriek followed shriek in rapid succession. The bed-clothes fell in a heap by the side of the bed— she was dragged by her long silken hair completely on to it again. Her beautiful rounded limbs quivered with the agony of her soul. The glassy, horrible eyes of the figure ran over that angelic form with a hideous satisfaction—horrible profanation. He drags her head to the bed's edge. He forces it back by the long hair still entwined in his grasp. With a plunge he seized her neck in his fang-like teeth—a gush of blood, and a hideous sucking noise follows. The girl has swooned, and the vampire is at his hideous repast!

With this book Prest had advanced the cause of vampire fiction immeasurably and it was to remain popular for many years, running into various editions as the century passed. As an achievement in the genre it stood pre-eminent in its horrible fascination for sophisticated and naïve Victorian readers alike. It was the immediate forerunner of one of the most famous characters of fiction but ironically was to be extinguished and almost forgotten by the success of an Irish author and theatre manager.

The man was, of course, Bram Stoker and his terrifying creation Count Dracula was to join such immortals of literature as Sherlock Holmes and the Three Musketeers. That Stoker's book itself was not particularly well-written was an irony that time has only sharpened. Count Dracula as a character in the novel and later the cinema was to unleash the floodgates of a genre that shows no sign of flagging popularity in the late twentieth century. We shall examine the writer and his creation in the next two chapters.

NINE

𝔅ram 𝔖toker's 𝔍mmortal ℭreation

BRAM STOKER was born Abraham Stoker in 1847 in County Dublin, the son of a country clergyman, the Reverend Abraham Stoker. In those leisurely, spacious days in Ireland the family lived in some style. A neighbouring estate was occupied by the Reverend Stoker's old friend, Colonel Deane, whose grandson Hamilton was later to adapt the younger Stoker's most famous work as a stage play which had success on a world scale. But these events were far ahead and indeed Stoker's early years were clouded with illness.

He was a sickly child and on several occasions medical men expressed doubts as to whether he would live to manhood. Despite these gloomy predictions of the Victorian doctors young Stoker flourished and eventually grew into a powerful, broad-shouldered man of abounding energy, full of gaiety and natural Irish wit. A strange parent perhaps for the sombre activities of Count Dracula, but a trait often met with in the arts, where the most unexpected juxtapositions abound.

In later years Bram Stoker was a professor of English but his interest lay always in the theatre and he eventually became business manager to the great Victorian actor Sir Henry Irving. He was to stay with Irving for no less than twenty-seven years and very successfully ran London's Lyceum Theatre, which was the scene of Sir Henry's greatest triumphs. It is interesting to speculate that such dramas as *The Bells*, in which Sir Henry gave an agonised performance as the tortured Mathias, may have given

Stoker the idea of writing something of his own. Certainly, being brought into close contact with many of the most famous stage artistes of his day could not have been without effect.

There is a story that Stoker had a " too generous helping of dressed crab " at supper one night and the resultant nightmare gave birth to Dracula. That story has a touch of the legendary about it also and we need not take it too seriously.

Certainly, Stoker had long shown literary talent and as he was a charming and cultivated man who wined and dined frequently with literary as well as theatrical people, it is not too difficult to see that his companions' talk would have fallen on fertile ground. Stoker had in fact published many novels and short stories before the work which was to make his name, and if he had curbed some of the excesses all too common among Victorian novelists, he might well have been one of the greatest masters of the English short story in the field of the macabre.

One has only to think of such tales as " The Judge's House ", " The Squaw " and the extraordinary " The Burial of the Rats " to realise his genuine power to terrify and appal his readers. These stories, and one or two others, are constantly in print today in various anthologies, and that they continue to horrify in an age which has seen many dreadful events must single Stoker out as an accomplished minor master.

" The Burial of the Rats " is worth a passing mention as evidence of Stoker's undoubted literary skill, though the pruning of one or two passages would improve it still further for the modern reader. It forms part of a collection first published by Stoker's widow in 1914. It tells the story of a young tourist who. falls among the rag-pickers of the Paris of 1850. The hero of this nightmare tale wanders among the wilderness of dustheaps and rubbish tips that then made up the far-flung suburb of Montrouge and, in passages as strange and dream-like as the images in a film by Antonioni, occupies his day until dusk begins to fall.

In a series of carefully worked scenes Stoker's hero first engages in conversation with an old soldier and, uneasily finds first one and then another rag-picker silently joining the group outside an old hut. How the young man slowly comes to realise that the company intend to murder him in that lonely spot for his few valuables is conveyed economically and with a dry-mouthed terror that many a greater literary figure might envy.

The young man's horrifying pursuit by the human scarecrows among landscapes as arid as the moon and his increased fear as he takes to water and then finds his stealthy pursuers are following him by row-boat remains a high-point of its kind in horror fiction. I rate this as one of the best macabre stories ever written and Arrow Books reprinted it in an excellent collection, *Dracula's Guest,* in 1966, following its clothbound publication by Jarrolds. The nine stories of Stoker's in the volume, of which the title story, " The Burial of the Rats ", together with " The Squaw " and " The Judge's House " are outstanding, convey a vivid impression of Stoker's range and limitations—as evidenced in the more pedestrian of the stories.

Certainly, he found such quality as described difficult to sustain in a work as lengthy as *Dracula,* which, despite its many flaws, must still be considered his masterpiece. That Stoker succeeded in immortalising himself with this novel was heavily against the odds, but today Count Dracula, together with Frankenstein and Sherlock Holmes, remains one of the three most invoked characters in English literature.

We shall consider *Dracula* and its place in vampire fiction a little later; when Stoker came to write it he was past fifty years of age and it must have seemed unlikely, to say the least, that the jovial theatre manager would ever really distinguish himself beyond writing pot-boilers like *The Lair of the White Worm* which, however, had considerable popular success and must have brought him in a fairly comfortable income.

He was in the habit of spending holidays at Cuden Bay on the coast of Scotland and much of *Dracula*'s 400 or so pages were composed at this spot. When the work was first published in 1897 *Dracula* proved a phenomenal success and Stoker found himself an international celebrity. Rider and Company, Stoker's principal publishers for many years, claimed as far back as the mid-nineteen-forties that the work had already sold more than a million copies which was an incredible circulation by the standards of the time.

And this was before the days when films on the Dracula-theme were arriving in the cinemas every few months; in the last thirty years or so, reliable figures are lacking, but with translation on a world-wide scale and the mass circulation of cheap paperback editions, Stoker's figures must have at least trebled since Rider made that impressive claim. They advertised it as " The world's most horrible thriller" and there is some justification for their statement.

Although their dust jacket is modest by comparison with blurb writer's pronouncements of the seventies, it states soberly and with truth, "Nothing in English fiction can compare with this novel of the vampire world and none has excited greater comment among the reviewers. Mr. Bram Stoker did not invent the idea of the Vampire—it is as old as the human race and is to be encountered in the histories of all countries. Anybody reading this story will get an indelible impression of the awful possibilities by which human existence is surrounded."

This is precisely the point of Stoker's novel and the fascination mentioned was one which was obviously felt by readers of all ages, who may well have been quite blase in other directions. As we have endeavoured to show in the course of this book the vampire, as a legendary being, as a fictional character, or as an unfortunate medical case, has an equal appeal to those who may be quite incurious about other aspects of superstition or criminal behaviour. Stoker's good fortune was to select the theme—for none of his other books, some of them every bit as sensational—have come down to us at a distance of some seventy-four years with such undiminished vigour.

Stoker undoubtedly enjoyed the celebrity the work secured for him and must have been an extremely happy and fulfilled man, both in the two phases of his professional life and in his own family background. One of his last literary acts—he died in 1912 at the comparatively early age of 65—was to prepare a series of his short macabre stories for publication. He dedicated one of these, *Dracula's Guest*, to his son but it was the last sad task of his wife to see the book through the press in 1914, after the death of her husband.

Florence Bram Stoker wrote in the preface to the original edition,

A few months before the lamented death of my husband—I might even say as the shadow of death was over him—he planned three series of short stories for publication, and the present volume is one of them. To his original list of stories in this book, I have added an hitherto unpublished episode from Dracula. It was originally excised owing to the length of the book, and may prove of interest to the many readers of what is considered my husband's most remarkable work.

The other stories have already been published in English and American periodicals. Had my husband lived longer, he might have seen fit to revise this work, which is mainly from the earlier years of his strenuous life. But, as fate has entrusted to me the issuing of it, I consider it fitting and proper to let it go forth practically as it was left by him.

The fragment, " Dracula's Guest ", is extremely interesting indeed and would have greatly strengthened *Dracula* if Stoker had left it in and used his pencil on some of the later, more protracted passages involving the two girls in the novel. We shall be considering " Dracula's Guest " when we come to the short story form. We shall now examine Stoker's tale at some length and try to pinpoint some of the reasons why it should be considered a masterwork in the literature of the vampire and one which has spawned literally hundreds of imitations. Dracula, in truth, lives for ever.

TEN

Enter Count Dracula

BRAM STOKER'S most famous work starts in the most innocuous way imaginable, reinforced by the somewhat dull and pedestrian method the author used to set out his chapters. This long and meandering novel is divided up into extracts from the hero Jonathan Harker's journal and from letters exchanged between the two pasteboard heroines, Harker's fiancée Mina Murray and her friend Lucy Westenra. Though Stoker is extremely ingenious for his time—one chapter for instance, is " Dr. Seward's Phonograph Diary, spoken by van Helsing "—the procedure adopted is an extremely arid one and makes the novel less lively in the more domestic passages than it otherwise might have been.

The book was dedicated " To my Dear Friend HOMMY-BEG ", which puzzled many people of a later generation as the publishers let the original dedication stand. The curious nomenclature was in the ancient Manx language, the dedicatee being the famous playwright and author Sir Hall Caine, a native of the Isle of Man, whose most famous novel was *The Manxman*.

Dracula opens with passages from Jonathan Harker's journal as the young solicitor is travelling in Transylvania to effect a property purchase for a titled client. The early chapters have the faded charm of a travelogue and increase the feeling of claustrophobic horror as the commonplace details of the journey gradually give way to the hinted terrors of the wild country in which the hero finds himself. This is where we first come across Bistritz, the post-town which Harker's client, Count Dracula, has given as a reference point, and which has served film makers and writers so well over the past seventy years.

At the Golden Krone Hotel Harker finds a letter from the Count which admirably sets the tone for much which follows.

" My Friend—Welcome to the Carpathians. I am anxiously expecting you. Sleep well tonight. At three tomorrow the diligence will start for Bukovina; a place on it is kept for you. At the Borgo Pass my carriage will await you and will bring you to me. I trust that your journey from London has been a happy one, and that you will enjoy your stay in my beautiful land. Your friend, Dracula."

In the morning Harker is warned by the landlord's wife that " It is the eve of St. George's Day " when the evil things of the world hold sway. She presses a crucifix into his hand and Harker, good Englishman that he is, does not wish to offend her, so he hangs it round his neck. On the coach the other travellers are talking about Harker and mumbled words he translates with the aid of his dictionary resolve themselves into such disquietening omens as witch, hell and Satan.

In a long and evocative passage describing Harker's coach journey Stoker rises to a very respectable level of descriptive prose and these scenes are among the most impressive in the book, setting the stage with great care for the charnel horrors to come. At the dark Borgo Pass Harker's driver rapidly abandons him as a sombre coach drawn by coal-black horses glides up. The taciturn coachman conveys Harker towards his destination at a lethal gait and there is an effective moment when wolves form a ring round the coach and keep pace with it.

Harker says:

This was all so strange and uncanny that a dreadful fear came upon me and I was afraid to speak or move. The time seemed interminable as we swept on our way, now in almost complete darkness, for the rolling clouds obscured the moon. We kept on ascending, with occasional periods of swift descent, but in the main always ascending. Suddenly I became conscious of the fact that the driver was in the act of pulling up the horses in the courtyard of a vast ruined castle, from whose tall black windows came no ray of light, and whose broken battlements showed a jagged line against the moonlit sky.

The Count's entrance, long delayed, is described by Stoker as follows.

Then there was the sound of rattling chains and the clanking of massive bolts drawn back. A key was turned with the loud grating noise of long disuse, and the great door swung back.

Within, stood a tall old man, clean-shaven save for a long white moustache, and clad in black from head to foot, without a single speck of colour about him anywhere. He held in his hand an antique silver lamp, in which the flame burned without chimney or globe of any kind, throwing long, quivering shadows as it flickered in the draught of the open door. The old man motioned me in with his right hand with a courtly gesture, saying in excellent English, but with a strange intonation—" Welcome to my house! Enter freely and of your own will!"

He made no motion of stepping to meet me, but stood like a statue, as though his gesture of welcome had fixed him into stone. The instant, however, that I had stepped over the threshold he moved impulsively forward, and holding out his hand grasped mine with a strength which made me wince, an effect which was not lessened by the fact that it seemed as cold as ice—more like the hand of a dead than a living man.

Harker dines on roast chicken, cheese and salad and " a bottle of old Tokay ", but the Count excuses himself from joining in as he has dined already. By this time the solicitor has had time to study his host in more detail and Stoker gives us this effective portrait.

His face was a strong—a very strong—aquiline, with high bridge of the thin nose and peculiarly arched nostrils; with lofty domed forehead and hair growing scantily round the temples, but profusely elsewhere. His eyebrows were very massive, almost meeting over the nose, and with bushy hair that seemed to curl in its own profusion. The mouth, so far as I could see it under the heavy moustache, was fixed and rather cruel-looking, with peculiarly sharp white teeth; these protruded over the lips, whose remarkable ruddiness showed astonishing vitality in a man of his years. For the rest, his ears were pale and at the tops extremely pointed; the chin was broad and strong, and the cheeks firm though thin. The general effect was one of extraordinary pallor.

Hitherto I had noticed the backs of his hands as they lay on his knees in the firelight, and they had seemed rather white and fine; but seeing them now close to me, I could not but notice that they were rather coarse—broad, with squat fingers. Strange to say, there were hairs in the centre of the palm. The nails were long and fine, and cut to a sharp point. As the Count leaned over me and his hands touched me, I could not repress a shudder. It may have been that his breath was rank, but a horrible feeling of nausea came over me, which do what I would, I could not conceal. The Count, evidently noticing it, drew back; and with a grim sort of smile, which showed more than he had yet done his protuberant teeth, sat himself down again on his own side of the fireplace.

There is silence for a moment and then comes the howling of wolves from far down the valley which elicits the comment from the Count, " Listen to them—the children of the night. What music they make!". And when Harker seems nonplussed by this, he adds: " Ah, sir, you dwellers in the city cannot enter into the feelings of the hunter."

Stoker wisely leaves the situation at this enigmatic exchange between the two men and goes on to describe Harker's next few days in the castle; the Count is away on business during the day and the visitor has the great place to himself. There are meals set for him, but no servants visible and he notes the lack of a mirror or toilet glass in his room. The Count returns at nightfall and Harker is surprised to learn that he speaks English fluently and understands all the colloquialisms. The pair have many conversations together and the Count tells him he may go anywhere in the castle, except where doors are locked. Harker then transacts the business which has brought him to Transylvania and conveys to the Count the deeds to an estate of Carfax near Purfleet.

Even by the standards of Victorian times it sounds a far from desirable property, being near to a church or chapel and a very large house close to it " formed into a private lunatic asylum ". Ideal for the Count however, who merely remarks that " to live in a new house would kill me "! Glancing over a map of England the Count has been annotating, Harker finds he has ringed the estate he has just purchased and that there are other marks indicating Exeter and Whitby.

The two long, atmospheric chapters which open the book are almost finished and Stoker introduces his first master-stroke; small details but ones which indicate the coming chill. The first is an effective scene where the Count comes up behind Harker while he is shaving; the young solicitor sees no reflection in the mirror and understandably startled, cuts himself. The Count is transfixed at the sight of blood and makes a grab at him but his hand comes in contact with the crucifix and he recoils. He hurls the glass out of the window and shatters it on the courtyard below. A short while later Harker finds the castle is on the edge of a precipice a thousand feet high and that all the doors are locked and bolted, making him the Count's prisoner.

Harker's journal continues the cat-and-mouse story of his relations with the Count, who behaves as though nothing has happened, spending long parts of each night recounting aspects of Transylvanian history to his young captive. For his part Harker dare not voice his fears and suspicions to the Count and confides them to his diary. An interesting point here is that Stoker narrates something of the true history of the genesis of his story, a certain Count Drakula, a Voivode or military governor, who was noted for his cruelty and barbarous deeds in medieval times. A tinge of humour, however, lightens the narrative when Harker wryly observes that his diary is like the *Arabian Nights*, as everything has to break off at cockcrow. The Count, naturally, makes his excuses to his guest and disappears with the coming of dawn.

But there is a method in the host's apparently inconsequential conversations; all the time he is asking Harker details about business in England and how he might deal with various affairs regarding his new property. He also requests Harker to write to his friends in England to tell them he is staying on with the Count for a further month.

Stoker skilfully prepares his most horrifying effects with passages of quiet, almost banal incident. One of the former occurs soon after. Harker is going to bed early for once and pauses on the stone staircase to look out from his prison and to get a breath of fresh air.

Stoker vividly continues:

I looked over the beautiful expanse, bathed in soft yellow moonlight till it was almost as light as day. In the soft light the distant hills became melted, and the shadows in the valleys and gorges of velvety blackness. The mere beauty seemed to cheer me; there was peace and comfort in every breath I drew. As I leaned from the window my eye was caught by something moving a storey below me, and somewhat to my left, where I imagined, from the lie of the rooms, that the windows of the Count's own room would look out.

The window at which I stood was tall and deep, stone-mullioned, and though weather-worn was still complete; but it was evidently many a day since the case had been there. I drew back behind the stonework, and looked carefully out. What I saw was the Count's head coming out from the window. I did not see the face, but I knew the man by the neck and the movement of his back and arms. In any case, I could not mistake the hands, which I had had so many opportunities of studying. I was at first interested and somewhat amused, for it is wonderful how small a matter will amuse and interest a man when he is a prisoner. But my very feelings changed to repulsion and terror when I saw the whole man slowly emerge from the window and begin to crawl down the castle wall over that dreadful abyss, face down, with his cloak spreading out around him like great wings.

The author achieves and maintains a high pitch of terror here and the finest moments and the most exciting sequences are contained within the first four or five chapters of the novel, which is why I have dwelt on the opening of the book at such length. For it is on the evocative introduction of this unique novel that its high reputation rests and it does not disappoint; *Dracula* would be worthwhile for these sequences alone.

With the shock of such episodes—for Harker sees the Count go out again the same way " like a lizard " a few nights later, Stoker's first great climax is upon us. Despite the Count's warning, the bored young man wanders into a forbidden part of the castle; there he feels sleepy and suddenly awakening finds three lovely young girls gliding towards him; one, a fair woman approaches him and Harker pretends sleep, anticipating that the girl will kiss him.

He says, " The fair girl advanced and bent over me till I could feel the movement of her breath upon me. Sweet it was in one sense, honey-sweet, and sent the same tingling through the nerves as her voice, but with a bitter underlying the sweet, a bitter offensiveness, as one smells in blood." The girl bends over him voluptuously and is about to fasten her teeth in his throat when the Count bursts in in a storm of fury and hurls the woman from him.

Harker adds, " His eyes were positively blazing. The red light in them was lurid, as if the flames of hell-fire blazed behind them. His face was deathly pale, and the lines of it were hard like drawn wires; the thick eyebrows that met over the nose now seemed like a heaving bar of white-hot metal."

He tells the women that Harker belongs to him and they reply, " Are we to have nothing?" Dracula gives them a bag from which comes " a low wail, as of a half-smothered child ". Stoker skilfully brings this horrific incident to a close as Harker faints.

He later awakes in his own room with the knowledge that he has been saved by the Count for some more awful fate; he still continues a prisoner and when Dracula asks him to write three letters indicating different stages of his journey home and each bearing a different date, he knows his days are numbered. The author of this evocative classic of horror fiction shows himself a master of suspense time and again as Harker's hopes of escape rise, each time only to be dashed. When a band of gypsies camp in the Count's courtyard he throws them letters, including one to Mina in shorthand which explains his situation. The gypsies however, hand them to Dracula, who takes them back to Harker. The Count becomes angry when he sees the shorthand and comments, " It is not signed. Well! so it cannot matter to us " and he calmly burns it.

The gypsies prepare to leave and load great boxes of earth on to their wagons, boxes which Harker later comes to realise contain the earth which will sustain the vampire, Dracula, on his journey to London, carrying the plague of vampirism to the wider world.

In great fear of death Harker recalls that the Count only appears after dark and prepares to seek him in daylight. He climbs from his window and after a hair-raising scramble succeeds in escaping from his room; in a deep vault of the castle he finds the body of the Count lying in one of the boxes of newly dug earth. Overcoming his horror Harker searches his clothes for the keys to the outer door but in vain. A day or two later, in great desperation Harker returns to the vault and attempts to destroy Dracula by striking his face with a shovel.

But, he says,

As I did so the head turned and the eyes fell upon me, with all their blaze of basilisk horror. The sight seemed to paralyse me and the shovel turned in my hand and glanced from the face, merely making a deep gash above the forehead. The shovel fell from my hand across the box, and as I pulled it away the flange of the blade caught the edge of the lid, which fell over again, and hid the horrid thing from my sight. The last glimpse I had was of the bloated face, bloodstained and fixed with a grin of malice which would have held its own in the nethermost hell.

As the gypsies leave the castle, with the living corpse of Dracula set to bring unknown terrors to an unsuspecting England, Harker still a prisoner, prepares to meet his death. Stoker had carried the Victorian horror novel to its highest peak in an inimitable opening which it would be hard to better, even today.

Unfortunately, as often happens, nothing which follows in the novel quite reaches the heights of terror achieved by these early chapters. A great deal of the correspondence between Lucy Westenra and Mina Murray is tedious in the extreme. There is no doubt that much of Stoker's long and involved book is very badly and sloppily written yet such is the fascination of its theme and the excellence of its best passages, that it still somehow survives. Stoker, however, has still to introduce one of his most interesting characters; apart from Dracula, Abraham van Helsing, who acts the Sherlock Holmes to the Count's Moriarty, is a well-rounded and sympathetic character who stands for Christianity and strength against the powers of darkness and the anti-Christ. If only the remaining personalities in the book had been as well-drawn, it might well have been literature, but perhaps that is asking for too much.

The ramblings and outdated slang of another pasteboard character, the young American Quincey P. Morris, are hard to take also but the determined reader who ploughs through these lengthy middle passages, which Stoker should have drastically pruned, is well rewarded with the finale. A sub-plot concerns Dr. Seward and his observations of the patient Renfield in the lunatic asylum at Purfleet—which adjoins Dracula's new house, it will be remembered—and these give the middle chapters more interest than they might otherwise have held. Like many workers in the genre Stoker was more at home with atmospheric terror and ill at ease in the romantic and domestic passages, which were more germane to any Victorian pot-boiler.

The story quickens with the excitingly described account of the arrival of Dracula's sailing vessel at Whitby and the discovery of the crew aboard dead and drained of blood. Stoker inserts an ingenious " flash-back " when the authorities read the vessel's log which tells a story of mounting fear among the crew as something from the " load of clay " in the hold attacks and gradually destroys those aboard.

These are the genuinely imaginative touches which lift the narrative above the merely pedestrian level but it is as well to emphasise that after the excellent beginning, these flashes of inspired writing are peaks sticking up from increasingly dull patches.

Stoker alternates these passages with apparently disconnected fragments of Dr. Seward's diary, which anticipate Resnais and Robbe-Grillet and the latter-day French cinema with their " montage " effect, which only make sense during the later stages of the book. One such is the chapter describing the lunatic Renfield eating spiders and other insects. In his strait-jacket he says, with chilling effect, " I shall be patient, Master. It is coming—coming —coming! "

In the meantime Lucy has been sleep-walking at Whitby and has been attacked by a mysterious illness, though the reader is in no doubt that the Count has commenced work in that fine old seaside resort. Mina then receives word that Jonathan is ill in a hospital run by nuns in Budapest and hurries to his side. All this and the book is less than a third through!

The remainder of the plot may be briefly summarised. Mina and Jonathan are married and return home; Renfield becomes worse in his delusions and then Dr. Seward is called from his asylum to attend Lucy. He is, fortunately, a friend of the great Professor Abraham van Helsing of Amsterdam who is summoned to attend Lucy.

Van Helsing's great duel with Count Dracula forms the remainder of the book and for those who have never read Stoker's original, it would be unfair to reveal the entire plot in detail. There is no doubt in my mind that the author's introduction of van Helsing is the decisive factor in saving the remaining pages from banality for the entire interest lies in watching the battle between van Helsing's scientific Christianity and the powers of outer darkness.

It is difficult at this distance in time to realise the impact all this must have made on its Victorian audience and some of Stoker's passages are strong stuff, even by today's standards.

Renfield, of course, who is another of the book's more interesting characters, because more strongly drawn, is a tool of the Count's; also involved in the plot complications are a savage wolf's escape from a zoo; and further vampiric attacks on Lucy with many blood-transfusion operations performed manfully by van Helsing and vividly described by Stoker. As Lucy hovers between life and death—she seems subject to mysterious attacks nearly every other page—van Helsing grows in stature until one can almost see the shadow of Peter Cushing reaching out across a gap of nearly sixty years before the fictional van Helsing matches with the actor on the screen.

All this time there has been no sign of Dracula and Stoker screws up the tension by describing the deaths of Lucy and her mother and the preparations for a joint funeral.

Says Seward, " There is peace for her at last. It is the end! " van Helsing tells him, " Not so; alas! Not so. It is only the beginning! "

Van Helsing himself is not described by the author until almost two hundred pages of closely packed type have been devoured. He is

a man of medium height, strongly built, with his shoulders set back over a broad, deep chest and a neck well balanced on the trunk as the head is on the neck. The poise of the head strikes one at once as indicative of thought and power; the head is noble, well-sized, broad, and large behind the ears. The face, clean-shaven, shows a hard, square chin, a large resolute, mobile mouth, a good-sized nose, rather straight, but with quick, sensitive nostrils, that seem to broaden as the big, bushy eyebrows come down and the mouth tightens. The forehead is broad and fine, rising at first almost straight and then sloping back above two bumps or ridges wide apart; such a forehead that the reddish hair cannot possibly tumble over it, but falls naturally back and to the sides. Big, dark blue eyes are set widely apart and are quick and tender or stern with the man's moods.

There is an awful fascination in the last third of the book, which rises with gripping momentum to one of the best climaxes in all Victorian fiction and does much to explain Dracula's perennial popularity. Van Helsing comes into his own in these big scenes, notably a charnel interlude in the cemetery vault where he and Harker find Lucy's coffin empty; and of course, in the final confrontations with the Count. The book is so constructed that it is easy to see why it has been such a popular subject for dramatisation on stage and later for the screen.

The sections dealing with the maniac Renfield too are shrewdly observed from a medical point of view and have a certain sombre power, as well as keeping the contemporary reader guessing. Incredibly, Stoker delays the Count's second entrance into the narrative until something like 200 pages have passed since we last saw him at Castle Dracula with Harker! But his presence has been hinted at throughout in diary entries, newspaper cuttings and with other ingenious devices of Stoker's, which says much for the vitality of his writing.

His methods, with climax after climax, would pall on stage or in the cinema, but they seem perfectly appropriate to his purpose and the later passages of *Dracula* achieve almost the same effect on the modern reader as they must have done in Victorian days. One must take the dross with the gold in order to achieve the full flavour of this unique novel; Stoker's value is that his achievement still remains unrivalled in his own field and it seems fairly safe to say that another century still might roll away before the Count's image grows dim in contemporary folklore.

Stoker's vampire, like his legendary counterpart has, true to type, drawn his nourishment from generation after generation of readers to live on in a form of immortality which would surely have astonished that good family man and bon viveur, Bram Stoker.

ELEVEN

The Dead Travel Fast: Themes in the Short Story

As THE reader may have noted it is difficult to wander far from Bram Stoker when considering the vampire theme in literature. So it is apposite to commence a study of the vampire in the short story form with some consideration of " Dracula's Guest ". This, as I indicated earlier, was a section of the novel *Dracula* which Stoker excluded from his original draft and which was not issued until after his death.

It was first published in 1914, re-issued in a special souvenir edition in 1927 and Hutchinson published it yet again as the title story in a collection of Stoker's macabre tales in paperback in 1966, about the same time that Jarrolds issued a clothbound edition. " Dracula's Guest ", which is well worth study, stands up as a self-contained short story and is, in fact, superior to some parts of the original book.

It sees Jonathan Harker out for a drive in Munich, presumably at some stage of his journey to Castle Dracula; before leaving, the manager of his hotel, the " Four Seasons ", warns him and the coachman to be back before nightfall, as it is Walpurgis Night. These passages are very similar to Harker's departure from the inn at Bistritz when he was warned by the landlord's wife that it was the Eve of St. George's Day so we may suppose that Stoker felt it too reminiscent of the material he was to use later. If so, this was a pity as the story is far more vivid than some of the passages which were retained.

Harker remains the same foolhardy hero of the novel, however, as the coach eventually comes to a deserted side road, down which the young solicitor wishes to drive. The coachman refuses and indicates a crucifix at the roadside and Harker realises that this is a spot where suicides were buried in former times; the sun goes in, it gets cold and a yelping bark in the distance, which Harker supposes to be a dog, sends the old chill down the reader's spine. Eventually Harker, as one would imagine, orders the cowardly coachman home and sets off on a brisk walk which he supposes will do him good.

He looks after the coach and a tall, thin man crosses the top of the hill at which the horses scream with terror and bolt back towards Munich; how much wiser than Harker the animals are! When he looks again both coach and thin man have disappeared. Harker walks for hours and eventually is overtaken by night and a snowstorm; wolves begin to howl again and he takes shelter in a grove of cypresses, only to find himself in front of a white marble sepulchre.

Stoker is at the top of his form in the description he gives of the scene:

Impelled by some sort of fascination, I approached the sepulchre to see what it was, and why such a thing stood alone in such a place. I walked around it, and read, over the Doric door, in German:

COUNTESS DOLINGEN OF GRATZ

IN STYRIA

SOUGHT AND FOUND DEATH

1801

On the top of the tomb, seemingly driven through the solid marble —for the structure was composed of a few vast blocks of stone— was a great iron spike or stake. On going to the back I saw, graven in great Russian letters:

" The dead travel fast "

Both the engravings on the tomb and the detail of the spike driven through it are master-strokes and Stoker achieves here a genuine thrill of terror which comes home to the reader even in a comfortable armchair in the warmth of his own home. If only he could have achieved this felicitous choice of imagery in the novel. Strangely enough, " Dracula's Guest ", precisely because it is short, strikes and maintains a high pitch of fear throughout and yet seems to avoid the Victorian Gothic with which much of

Dracula is cluttered. The writing here seems more modern in style and because the phrasing is more polished than many of *Dracula*'s rougher passages, carries more conviction.

Harker realises he is in deadly danger on Walpurgis Nacht. Huddled in the doorway of the tomb he is conscious of the wolves closing in on him through the numbing cold. As his senses leave him he realises that an animal like a great dog is crouching on him and licking his throat.

In a finale in which tension and surprise are nicely blended Harker is rescued by a troop of cavalry, who shoot at the wolf which has been lying on him. There is blood on the marble of the vault entrance but it is not Harker's; he is told that the wolf lying on him has kept him warm and has saved his life.

In a snatch of soldier's dialogue, Stoker makes one of the troopers say of the wolf, " No use trying for him without the sacred bullet."

Safely back at the Four Seasons Harker wonders at his timely rescue and the manager hands him a message. It reads; " Be careful of my guest—his safety is most precious to me. Should aught happen to him, or if he be missed, spare nothing to find him and ensure his safety. He is English and therefore adventurous. There are often dangers from snow and wolves and night. Lose not a moment if you suspect harm to him. I answer your zeal with my fortune. Dracula."

Curiously, the nineteenth century's finest writer of macabre stories and almost certainly the greatest stylist in the field, Edgar Allan Poe seems never to have written a true vampire story, though his morbid imagination encompassed burial alive, which was almost an obsession with him, necrophilism and the return of the dead; possibly " Ligeia ", a decadent masterpiece in the true sense, was the nearest thing to it; the return from the dead of the hero's lost love Ligeia, taking the place of the dying wife Rowena.

Even that other great stylist Henry James tried his hand at the vampire theme in his short stories from time to time, but the topic was so delicately and so elusively evoked in the master's elliptical prose and qualified clauses that it really lies outside this study. It was left to the nineteenth century's most gifted short story writer and arguably the world's greatest master of this form, Guy de Maupassant to create in " The Horla " one of the most horrific and memorable vampiric presences in the whole of literature.

In his short life de Maupassant created no less than seven novels and over 300 short stories, and almost all of this remarkable output could be classed as literature with a capital L, though much of his work is, inevitably, of uneven quality. Born in 1850 he was a friend and pupil of Flaubert, and became well known as a journalist, author and acid wit in the Paris of the 1880s. A handsome man of boundless energy he was a great womaniser and gourmet and squandered his gifts in debauchery and endless socialising.

Axel Munthe gives a vivid picture of de Maupassant in his famous book *The Story of San Michele* and says that the celebrated French writer's thoughts were seldom far from death. Munthe spent two days as a guest on de Maupassant's yacht the *Bel Ami* at anchor off Antibes. Munthe says the writer was gathering materials on insanity for " The Horla " and told the Swedish doctor that he wished to die in the arms of a woman; the latter felt he was already far along the road to doing so.

Munthe wrote of the man his friends called " *le taureau triste* ", " He was still producing with feverish haste one masterpiece after another, slashing his excited brain with champagne, ether and drugs of all sorts. Women after women in endless succession hastened the destruction."

He died of syphilis at the early age of 43 in 1893 at an asylum in Passy on the outskirts of Paris. The talented American writer Manuel Komroff movingly re-created de Maupassant's last days in his brilliant short story, " A Red Coat for Night ", which was published in England in 1944. In " The Horla " de Maupassant unwittingly drew a picture of his own fate.

The narrator of the story relates the incidents which occur to him in diary form but in de Maupassant's hands there could be no greater contrast to the effects he achieves compared with Stoker's domestic passages in *Dracula*.

He begins with quiet entries showing the narrator's pleasure at the house in which he was born and describes the tranquil passage of the Seine past his windows, bearing with it barges and private yachts. A few days later, however, he is fevered and depressed and on consulting his doctor for his nerves, continues to deteriorate, despite the medicines he is given. He opens his cupboards, looks under his bed and dreads nightfall.

Then:

I sleep—for some little time—two or three hours—then a dream—no, a nightmare, lays hold on me. I am quite aware that I am in bed and asleep—I feel it and know it—and I also feel that someone is drawing close to me, looking at me, feeling me, getting up on my bed, kneeling on my chest, taking my neck between his hands and squeezing . . . squeezing with all his strength . . . trying to strangle me.

And I struggle, bound down by that awful helplessness which paralyses us in dreams; I want to cry out—I cannot; I want to move—I cannot; with fearful efforts, gasping for breath, I try to turn over, to throw off this being who chokes and stifles me—I cannot!

Suddenly I wake, frantic, bathed in sweat. I light a candle. I am alone.

Seldom has there been a better description of a vampiric presence sucking the vitality from the sleeper, than in these masterly sentences. It is remarkable too, how closely they parallel the sensations of the victims of vampires in eighteenth-century Europe as described in Chapter Three; particularly of the terrible dreams; the sensation of weight; the sickness and suffocation suffered; and above all of the pressure on the chest and the perspiration.

Maupassant in his fabulous story, beautifully translated by Brian Rhys, describes the degeneration into madness of the author of the diary who gradually becomes conscious that a vampire is draining the vitality, the very life from his body. He says, " I wait for sleep as one might wait for the executioner."

The narrator embarks on a short holiday but returning to his house finds the old nightmares recurring. In a powerful passage of 4th July he relates, " A fresh attack, and no mistake! The old nightmares have come back. Last night I felt someone crouching on top of me, who, with his mouth to mine, was drinking my life through my lips. Yes, he was draining it out of my throat, as would a leech. Then he got off me, gorged, and I woke up."

On 5th July the hero of this remarkable story locks his bedroom door and on drinking half a glass of water notices that the water-bottle at his bedside is full to the glass stopper. He sleeps, but after two hours is awakened by a seizure more frightful than before.

" Imagine a man who is being assassinated in his sleep, who

awakes to find a knife in his lungs, and lies there covered with blood, with the death-rattle in his throat, unable to draw his breath, on the verge of death, understanding nothing at all."

Maupassant emphasises the horror of the situation when the hero finds the hitherto full water-bottle at his bedside completely empty; he realises that some being has drunk it during the night. The ensuing passages emphasise the narrator's growing paranoia as the water-bottle is drained night after night.

On 9th July, " I replaced the water and milk on my table by themselves, taking care to cover the bottles in white muslin, and to tie down the corks. Then I rubbed my lips, beard and hands, with black lead, and went to bed. The same inexorable sleep took possession of me, followed soon after by the horrible awakening. I hadn't stirred; the sheets themselves had no stain. I hastened to the table. The muslin covering the bottles remained spotless. I untied the strings, panting with fear. Every drop of water was drunk! Every drop of milk was drunk! Ah, God above!"

But the narrator is not insane; squabbles break out among the servants over glasses in the house being broken and in passages terrible in their simplicity the horrified hero of this classic master-piece one afternoon sees a rose in his garden broken from its stem by an invisible hand and hang in the air as though some unseen presence were sniffing its perfume. Later he sees the pages of a book in his room being quietly turned by the unknown persecutor whom he chases from the house.

He then reads in a scientific review that people in Rio de Janeiro have fled from their homes because of the attacks of a kind of vampire which feeds on them during their sleep and drinks water and milk during the night.

He observes, " Aha, I remember the lovely Brazilian three-master that passed below my windows on her way up the Seine, last 8th of May! I thought her so beautiful, so white, so pleasant! The Being was on board, coming from the land where his race was born! And he saw me! He saw my white house too; and he leaps from the ship to the shore. Ah, God above! And now I know, I foresee. Man's reign on earth is over."

He sits up waiting for the thing which is slowly sapping the life from him and which he comes to realise is called the Horla. He sends for a locksmith and orders iron shutters for his room. In a chillingly described duel of wits between the unseen vampire and de Maupassant's tortured hero, the finale comes when he sets fire to his own house in order to destroy the Horla. Finally, in the most unnerving passage of all, in which de Maupassant could have been describing his own disjointed existence, he observes, " No, no, no, no . . . there is no room for doubt, no doubt at all! He is not dead.

" Well then . . . well then . . . the only thing left to do is to kill—myself."

TWELVE

The Theme to Date

BEFORE THE nineteenth century was quite out a unique contribution to vampire lore in the short-story field was made by one of the greatest novelists of the macabre, whose work fits comfortably into none of the accepted moulds. Sheridan Le Fanu, the Irish master whose novel *Uncle Silas* is a classic in the field of terror, was underrated in his own lifetime and many critics still find it difficult to accept him into the canon of those who, perhaps of lesser achievement, are regarded as masters of literature.

This would not worry Le Fanu, who was a Dublin editor and newspaper proprietor for most of his working life; his achievements in journalism are long forgotten but, fortunately for lovers of the ghost story and the macabre, he created some of the most enduring and horrifying tales in the field of Gothic horror, which will always give him a small but important niche in the genre.

His short story " Green Tea " is described by the distinguished critic V. S. Pritchett as " among the best half-dozen ghost stories in the English language " and his collection, *In a Glass Darkly*, contains five long tales, all of which are of a high standard.

Curiously, Pritchett does not regard either of Le Fanu's novels, *Uncle Silas* or *The House by the Churchyard* very highly, though the former has one of the greatest scenes of terror ever created in the whole of English literature. With his short story " Carmilla ", Le Fanu penned one of the best of all vampire tales.

" Carmilla " is high Gothic at its best; as if to emphasise this aspect, the author mentions Gothic architecture several times on the very first page of his story, when setting the scene in an old Austrian schloss! " Carmilla " is, in fact, a novella of over sixty closely-packed pages of type, a length typical of this author, who was a great innovator at creating atmosphere in the Dickensian style, but without Dickens's studied " quaintness ".

" Carmilla " is presented as one of the case-studies of Le Fanu's character, the distinguished physician Dr. Martin Hesselius, and in fact all the stories of *In a Glass Darkly* have prologues which introduce them as being cases which the doctor has studied. Unlike many Victorian novelists, Le Fanu's writing is pithy and to the point and his prologues are admirably concise, usually a bare half dozen sentences.

Le Fanu carefully sketches in the milieu and the surroundings of the schloss in Styria—one wonders if his Karnsteins may not be related to the Countess Dolingen of Bram Stoker—and the desolation into which the area has fallen. The narrator of the story first relates a traumatic incident which befell him as a child when a young and pretty girl appears at his bedside and lies down beside him; soothing sleep turns to terror when, " I was wakened by a sensation as if two needles ran into my breast very deep at the same moment, and I cried loudly." The servants come running in at the child's screams but the girl has gone.

Some years later the narrator speaks of a friend of his father's, General Spielsdorf, who writes to say his much loved ward Bertha is dead and that he is seeking to " devote my remaining days to tracking and extinguishing a monster " who was responsible for her death. Later that night the narrator, his father and the two governesses are enjoying the moonlit beauty of the countryside surrounding the schloss when a carriage approaches and an accident occurs when its wheels run over the root of a lime tree.

A young girl travelling in the carriage is stunned and her mother severely shaken. The occupants of the schloss press their hospitality on the injured travellers. The mother leaves her beautiful daughter with the hero's father, promising to return in three months; she warns him that the daughter is in delicate health and nervous. The girl's name is Carmilla and she is of an old and noble family. Both the narrator and the girl are shocked when they meet; they had seen one another in a dream, twelve years before. The narrator recognises the girl who had appeared at his bedside when he was a child.

Le Fanu says of Carmilla that she was charming in most particulars but the young man of the story has some reservations; "There was a coldness, it seemed to me, beyond her years, in her smiling melancholy persistent refusal to afford me the least ray of light." He speaks here of the mystery of Carmilla's antecedents; he also notes her failure to rise every day until the early afternoon, and her bodily languor.

When a plague-fever seems to strike the village near the schloss, with two girls dying suddenly, both of whom appeared to have been attacked by some unnatural creature, Carmilla merely observes, "everyone must die; and all are happier when they do." A hunchback, a well-known mountebank, visits the castle to entertain and angers Carmilla by offering to file down the long, sharp tooth "like a needle" which he discerns when she smiles at him.

The fever round about seems to increase and other people are ill and dying when a picture cleaner arrives with some of the family portraits; one is of Mircalla Karnstein, painted in 1698, which turns out to be the absolute image of Carmilla. Le Fanu's sombre story draws to a close as the hero is again attacked by something in the night, which pierces his breast.

The general whose ward fell victim to a monster arrives at the Chateau and after a series of horrific incidents which reveal his perfect grasp of the macabre form, Le Fanu sets his final tableau in the old burial ground of the Karnsteins.

The grave of the Countess Mircalla was opened; and the General and my father recognised each his perfidious and beautiful guest, in the face now disclosed to view. The features, though a hundred and fifty years had passed since her funeral, were tinted with the warmth of life. Her eyes were open; no cadaverous smells exhaled from the coffin.

The two medical men, one officially present, the other on the part of the promoter of the inquiry, attested the marvellous fact that there was a faint but appreciable respiration, and a corresponding action of the heart. The limbs were perfectly flexible, the flesh elastic; and the leaden coffin floated with blood, in which to a depth of seven inches, the body lay immersed. Here then, were all the admitted signs and proofs of vampirism.

Le Fanu terminates his marvellously atmospheric story by having the Countess's head struck from her body and a sharp stake driven through her, in the classic tradition. The corpse is then placed on a pile of wood and reduced to ashes which are thrown in the river and borne away.

The story concludes, " The following spring my father took me a tour through Italy. We remained away for more than a year. It was long before the terror of recent events subsided; and to this hour the image of Carmilla returns to memory with ambiguous alternations—sometimes the playful, languid, beautiful girl; sometimes the writhing fiend I saw in the ruined church; and often from a reverie I have started, fancying I heard the light step of Carmilla at the drawing-room door."

Space precludes the mention of many other fine nineteenth-century stories of vampires; one of the best of its kind is the French writer Theophile Gautier's atmospheric " The Beautiful Vampire ", which relates the history of a young man who marries a girl who turns out to bear the taint of vampirism.

Following the great highlights of the Victorian age it was left to a few gifted short-story writers and novelists of the twentieth century to revivify the vampire legend in their work and to carry this most fascinating theme on to new planes, notably those of science fiction and futuristic literature. In a volume of this sort it is impossible to be definitive but we shall now note the most important contributions made from 1900 to the present day.

Three of the finest practitioners of the macabre story or what was then called the ghost tale, in the early twentieth century, were F. Marion Crawford, M. R. James and E. F. Benson. All brought considerable scholarship and erudition to their fiction, the result being that their works have little dated though in some cases more than fifty years have passed since the stories first appeared.

Montague Rhodes James was a Fellow of All Souls and passed his life in scholarly pursuits. He wrote macabre tales as a hobby, many of them being created in the mid and late 1890s, when they were published in magazines, though the majority were not seen in book form until the early years of this century. His most famous collection, *Ghost Stories of an Antiquary*, was published by Edward Arnold in 1904. His only work which hints of the vampire was " An Episode of Cathedral History "

James had a marvellous felicity for suggesting the unpleasant—one of his most frightful creations was a thing with teeth and a wet mouth into which the hero put his hand when FEELING UNDER HIS PILLOW. In one of his rare introductions to his collected stories, James vividly suggests his own imaginative qualities when he says,

> There may be possibilities, too, in the Christmas cracker, if the right people pull it, and if the motto which they find inside has the right message on it. They will probably leave the party early, pleading indisposition; but very likely a previous engagement of long standing would be the more truthful excuse.
>
> In parenthesis, many common objects may be made the vehicles of retribution, and where retribution is not called for, of malice. Be careful how you handle the packet you pick up in the carriage-drive, particularly if it contains nail-parings and hair. Do not, in any case, bring it into the house; it may not be alone.

Dr. James, a former Provost of Eton, in " An Episode of Cathedral History ", relates the story of an appalling " thing "— one of his particular specialities is not to define too closely the nature of the horror—which has lived on for centuries in an altar tomb in an ancient cathedral undergoing renovation. When a piece of paper is pushed through a crack in the stonework it is bitten off by something inside and the paper comes away wet and " black ".

James revels in atmosphere and the reader too cannot help being affected by the nastiness of the creature in the tomb, which finally escapes, bowling over several by-standers but not before someone has seen " a thing like a man, all over hair, and two great eyes to it ". One of James's most effective and remarkable stories and, like most of his work, extremely plausible in the telling.

Marion Crawford was early in the field with a magnificent vampire story, " For the Blood is the Life ", which appeared in his *Uncanny Tales* published by Benn as long ago as 1911.

For the " Blood is the Life " is one of the most original and unusual essays in the genre and is re-published frequently, having attained classic status. Unlike most works of this nature the action takes place in semi-tropical heat beneath the bronze skies of Calabria, where the owner of an ancient tower built to hold the Barbary pirates at bay, entertains a Swedish artist friend. As the pair dine on top of the tower, admiring the sunset over the sea, the artist is troubled by a small mound on the hillside which resembles a grave, and what appears to be a body lying on top of it.

Investigating by moonlight he finds the mound an optical illusion but his host, watching from the top of the tower, is horrified to see a transparent figure clinging to his friend's knees. As he walks back, the figure appears to give a cry and sinks back on top of the mound.

The host tells the guest a story of two workmen building an extension to a house in the nearby village, who steal a chest containing money from beneath a dying man's bed; burying it near the sea-shore they are surprised by a gypsy girl Cristina, who is in love with the dead man's son. She has seen their theft so they kill her and bury her with the money, intending to come back for it later.

When the son returns to his father's house he is penniless, his fiancée forsakes him as he has no settlement and he sinks into poverty and melancholy; returning from his work in the fields one day, he sees the form of Cristina who lures him down a path to the beach. He passes the night with her and he awakes on the cold earth at dawn, weak and debilitated. Powerless to resist the girl, who beckons to him night after night and drains the life from him, the young man is near death when he is rescued from his *la belle dame sans merci* by the caretaker of the tower, who has just returned from the mainland.

He seeks the help of the village priest and late at night they find the young man sprawled on the earth with blood trickling down his collar and " another face that looked up from the feast ". They dig up the stolen chest from Cristina's grave and Antonio, the caretaker, puts a stake through the thing in the pit. The priest, half-fainting, hears " the most awful sound of all— a woman's shriek, the unearthly scream of a woman neither dead or alive, but buried deep for many days ".

" For the Blood is the Life " is a beautifully realised story and unlike many vampire pieces from minor hands, will bear reading and re-reading; it conveys a genuine *frisson* of horror and is a small masterpiece in its field.

E. F. Benson (1867-1940), the son of a former Archbishop of Canterbury, made his name with stories of the macabre in the twenties with such fine collections as *The Room in the Tower and Other Stories*. His " Mrs. Amworth ", one of the most unusual as well as one of the most terrible vampire tales in all fiction, first appeared in his collection *Visible and Invisible*, in 1923.

" Mrs. Amworth " is highly original, but with a very different setting to Crawford's tale; one so ordinary that when the terrors come they are so unexpected that they shock all the more profoundly. The events of the story take place in a quiet Sussex village to which comes Mrs. Amworth, widow of an Indian civil servant who had been a judge in the North-west Provinces. She is returning home really, as her family had inhabited the village of Maxley for centuries.

She quickly becomes the centre of the social life of the neighbourhood and is well-liked by everyone but appears ill at ease in the presence of Francis Urcombe, a friend and neighbour of the narrator's, who has made a life-long study of the supernatural. He is particularly interested in vampirism, but makes an unfortunate gaffe when he tells Mrs. Amworth one evening that there was an outbreak of vampirism in her district in India. She denies it laughingly but when she has gone Urcombe, disturbed, tells his host that her husband had been a victim of the mysterious disease, as he calls it.

It is a hot summer in Maxley, with a plague of sharp, biting gnats and cases of illness are frequent; the symptoms include anaemic pallor and prostration, accompanied by drowsiness and abnormal appetite. A gardener's boy of about 17 is near death because of this, despite the fact that Mrs. Amworth frequently visits him with nourishing food.

She tells the narrator that she loves gardening and air and earth. She adds, " Positively I look forward to death, for then I shall be buried and have the kind earth all round me. No leaden caskets for me—I have given explicit instructions." The narrator leaves Mrs. Amworth but on retiring for the night is visited by terrible dreams, in which he is suffocating and in which he sees the vision of Mrs. Amworth's smiling face hanging outside each of his open windows.

Next day Urcombe visits his friend and says he is certain the gardener's boy is the victim of a vampire; he has given instructions for him to be moved to his own house, which causes Mrs. Amworth considerable surprise. Urcombe has the boy placed in one of his bedrooms with the window a little open and keeps watch; about midnight he hears something trying to open the window and sees the face of Mrs. Amworth floating 20 feet from the ground. She has her hand on the window frame and Urcombe suddenly slams the window down and catches the tip of her finger.

The two friends confer and Urcombe hints that Mrs. Amworth, frustrated in her intention of getting at the boy, had tried to attack the narrator. The two men keep continuous watch by the boy's bedside and he is getting better; two mornings later Mrs. Amworth comes along the road and the couple notice that one finger of her left hand is bandaged. She tells the two men that she has come to bring the patient a bowl of jelly and sit with him for an hour.

Benson's brilliant story continues:

Urcombe paused a moment, as if making up his mind, and then shot out a pointing finger at her.

" I forbid that," he said. " You shall not sit with him or see him. And you know the reason as well as I do."

I have never seen so horrible a change pass over a human face as that which now blanched hers to the colour of a grey mist. She put up her hand as if to shield herself from that pointing finger, which drew the sign of the cross in the air, and shrank back cowering on to the road. There was a wild hoot from a horn, a grinding of brakes, a shout—too late—from a passing car, and one long scream suddenly cut short. Her body rebounded from the roadway after the first wheel had gone over it, and the second followed. It lay there, quivering and twitching, and was still.

Mrs. Amworth is buried in the local cemetery a few days later but her presence has not gone from the village; in a climax compounded cleverly of ordinary, everyday description and the mounting terror of the events described, the vampire that is Mrs. Amworth is found in her grave and put to rest in the classical manner, though on this occasion Urcombe uses a pick-axe to perform the cleansing task. Benson's tale is one much relished by anthologists and is frequently re-printed to this day.

One of the most clever variants on the theme was " The Vampire " by Jan Neruda, which was widely published in the thirties. A very short tale, it concealed its sting in the final line, in the manner of O. Henry. On a steamer on the Bosphorus a mixed bag of passengers take stock of one another; a delicate, pale Polish girl who looks as though she is recovering from illness leans on the arm of her fiancé. A young Greek artist with long black curly hair down to his shoulders is also on the boat.

When the party, including the young couple, disembark and are admiring the view across the Sea of Marmora, the artist starts to draw on his pad; he later leaves and during the evening the Polish family hear him having a row with their landlord.

The young Pole engaged to the girl asks who the artist is. The landlord says bad-temperedly, " We call him the Vampire." He tells the appalled family that the man draws nothing but corpses and is ready with his death-mask the very same day.

" That's because he draws in advance . . . but the devil knows, he never makes a mistake."

The old Polish lady gives a shriek, the young girl collapses; the fiancé rushes down the steps and seizes the Greek painter's sketch-pad. From it falls the striking portrait of the young girl. " Her eyes were closed; a myrtle-wreath encircled her forehead ".

In stories like this the author hits home and there is genuine shock in such a denouement. In lighter vein—though his medical training gave him the expertise to shock through detailed description—Sir Arthur Conan Doyle had posed a problem for his celebrated detective, Mr. Sherlock Holmes, much earlier in the century.

But in " The Adventure of the Sussex Vampire " he makes it quite clear that he has no patience with such superstitions. The scene is set with quiet humour with the receipt by Holmes of a strait-laced letter from the solicitors Morrison, Morrison and Dodd. Headed prosaically, " Re Vampires ", it tells Holmes, " Our client, Mr. Robert Ferguson of Ferguson and Muirhead, tea brokers, of Mincing Lane, has made some inquiry from us in a communication of even date concerning vampires. As our firm specialises entirely upon the assessment of machinery the matter hardly comes within our purview."

Holmes is intrigued but when the faithful Watson consults the " great index volume ", he is disgusted with the information it gives on vampires.

" Rubbish, Watson, rubbish! What have we to do with walking corpses who can only be held in their graves by stakes driven through their hearts? It's pure lunacy."

But for once Watson is far wiser than the Master. He tells him, " But surely, the vampire was not necessarily a dead man? A living person might have the habit. I have read, for instance, of the old sucking the blood of the young in order to retain their youth."

And Holmes graciously retorts, " You are right, Watson. It mentions the legend in one of these references. But are we to give serious attention to such things. This agency stands flat-footed upon the ground, and there it must remain. The world is big enough for us. No ghosts need apply."

Despite Holmes's fears, however, the Sussex Vampire turns out to be one of his most fascinating cases. Ferguson, an old school friend of Watson's has married a South American girl as his second wife; Dolores had previously attacked his son by his first marriage, a crippled boy of 15 and was then seen by a nurse to have injured her own son, a small child a year old. On the second occasion she was caught by the husband drinking the child's blood.

The tale is one of Doyle's best, if we can forgive Holmes his slighting remark about vampires; and in a typically neat plot which is full of the usual paradoxes, Holmes solves the case and vindicates the lady's honour.

The crippled child is madly jealous of the new baby, which represents all that is strong and wholesome; he attacked his tiny step-brother by using a South American arrow tipped with curare. On both occasions the mother sucked the poison from the wound and saved the child's life but dare not tell her husband, who worshipped his crippled son.

Where we may quarrel with Holmes in this splendid adventure, however, is where he says to Ferguson, " The idea of a vampire was to me absurd."

England's greatest criminal detective was a little wanting in imagination on this occasion; had he lived some eighty or so years earlier he may well have been called in to investigate the bizarre and terrifying affair of Carmilla.

The American H. P. Lovecraft, perhaps the greatest master of the pure horror story this century has seen did not, regrettably, write any tales of vampiric terror so must be excluded from this survey. However, his friend and collaborator August Derleth, one of the most gifted and prolific writers of the macabre, author of more than a hundred books and founder of Arkham House, a unique publishing venture which produces nothing but macabre literature, well maintains the tradition.

Derleth, who not only published but completed many of Love-craft's fragmentary tales, left uncompleted at his early death, also writes under the pseudonym of Stephen Grendon and a number of memorable stories of vampirism have emanated from the Derleth/Grendon pen.

In one of his most famous pieces, "The Drifting Snow" Derleth as Stephen Grendon, in a narrative which is almost all atmosphere, relates the history of a servant girl who is driven out of a great house to die in the snow. She returns as a snow-vampire to lure others to their deaths, and in a finale, delicately and fastidiously written, as befits this outstanding writer, she claims yet another victim. Now there will be three figures standing in front of the house when it snows, which is why the old lady always keeps the west windows heavily curtained at night. A highly original variation on an ancient theme.

In his own persona August Derleth, in a very early tale, called "Bat's Belfry", chose another vampire theme, and boldly has his hero, Sir Harry Barclay discover an early copy of Stoker's *Dracula* in the opening paragraphs. Sir Harry lives on the English moors, in a place very like Doyle's Baskerville Hall. Sir Harry's pre-decessor, Baron Lohrville, called the house "Bat's Belfry" and during his time at the mansion a number of girls disappeared from the village. Later, Sir Harry's body is found drained of blood and in his journal he speaks of finding the Baron and a bevy of female vampires in the cellar.

The story is obviously prentice work which Derleth himself was not keen on seeing reprinted, but it is still highly entertaining for all that, and of great interest in view of Derleth's later develop-ment. And it is full of rich, derivative plums for the enthusiast of vampire fiction; Sir Harry's valet is called Mortimer—the reader will recall Mortimer, Sir Henry Baskerville's doctor in *The Hound of the Baskervilles*—and the appearance of the vampire Baron and the four girls is an echo of a similar theme in Stoker's *Dracula*. None the worse for that, of course, and the story is well worth the reading, something like forty years after its first appearance in print.

Derleth's output is so prolific in the short story field—he once wrote no less than seventeen first-class stories in one month, working late at night, his room full of students, after heavy days spent revising a major novel!—that it has not been possible for me to trace all of his stories which have a vampire theme. I understand there are a number of others. Significantly, the tales referred to above, originally written to the deadline of the famous American magazine *Weird Tales* and later collected under the title, *When Graveyards Yawn*, are all of outstanding quality; yet another tribute to August Derleth, an author unique both as a writer and as a human being.

Inevitably, as the century progressed, many lesser writers tried their hands at the vampire theme, with the result that satiation set in and the magazine market in particular was flooded with cheap, badly written stories which added little to the legend of Bram Stoker's striking original. The theme was used increasingly too, in ways which had little to do with its true origins. Herbert Jenkins, for example, published in the early twenties, James Corbett's adventure story " Vampire of the Skies ", which had an aviation background!

But the first-class writers continued to transmute the dross of the theme into the pure gold of imaginative fiction. H. G. Wells wrote a vampire short story of remarkably vivid horror in " The Flowering of the Strange Orchid ". Wedderburn, the orchid grower purchases an unusual species which had been collected by a young man who was found lying dead in a mangrove swamp. One of the orchids was under his body, which had been drained of blood by leeches.

Wedderburn tends his new orchid, which has strange, aerial roots, and in a finale custom-made for the cinema of horror is found unconscious and near death, clutched hard in the tentacles of the vampire-plant. He is rescued through the courage of his housekeeper. One of the very best of the vampire-variant tales, as might be imagined of a story from the brain of Wells.

Conan Doyle had dealt with a similar theme in " The Parasite " and other distinguished workers in the macabre who took the vampire legend as a basis for short stories, included Algernon Blackwood, one of the most impressive writers in this difficult medium. In his " The Strange Adventures of a Private Secretary in New York ", the hapless hero of this *tour de force* spends a night of terror in a mansion after applying for a position as secretary. He not only discovers that his new employer has a penchant for raw meat but other, more outrageous tastes, before the night is over. Not typical of Blackwood, the story is more genuinely frightening than much of Blackwood's gentle prose, the desperate situations being relieved by flashes of sardonic humour.

Among the most brilliant writers working in the field of the macabre today, mainly in America, a number have touched on the theme of the vampire, notably Ray Bradbury, the gifted poet of science-fiction; Robert Bloch, Manly Wade Wellman, Cornell Woolrich and Theodore Sturgeon.

Richard Mathieson is another modern writer who has made the legend of the vampire almost his own. In " No Such Thing as a Vampire ", he satirises the genre, using a doctor to take a horrible revenge on his wife and her lover. The doctor uses a syringe to take blood from his wife and after drugging the lover leaves him in a coffin so that the outraged peasantry can take their revenge.

In his novel, *I Am Legend*, definitely one for the specialist, Mathieson utilises vampirism with a science-fiction theme. The work presupposes that the hero is the last man on earth and at night barricades himself in his home against the screaming, blood-thirsty crowd outside. They all want to drink his blood, it seems, because all are vampires who had once been his friends and neighbours. Mathieson deserves high marks for originality and perhaps he is shrewder than he supposes, for haven't we all had friends and neighbours like that at one time or another?

Theodore Sturgeon is also an outstanding writer in the modern field. His novel *Some of Your Blood* appeared in 1961 and revealed striking originality, though some might have found the theme more than usually offensive in the way the author suggested the blood was obtained.

Other fine vampire stories which may be mentioned briefly include two more by E. F. Benson: " The Room in the Tower " and " And No Bird Sings ". The latter featured a horrifying slug-like creature which haunted a wood and sucked the life from rabbits and other small creatures, almost claiming the hero in one of the best finales of its kind ever committed to paper.

In the main tradition was Victor Roman's " Four Wooden Stakes ", a truly fiendish piece in the old *Weird Tales* form which had a finale featuring the destruction of no less than four vampires! The story was immensely popular and was included in Christine Campbell Thomson's famous *Not at Night* series of volumes in the thirties.

Robert Bloch's " Living Dead ", Cornell Woolrich's " My Lips Destroy ", Manly Wade Wellman's " The Devil is Not Mocked " are some of the new-style vampire stories that are well worth the connoisseur's time. They all share one thing with the vampire-tales of classical type: well-constructed plots, good writing and plausibility.

The difficulty today is to give a new shape to an old theme; this was a problem I faced in 1968 when I was invited by Peter Haining to contribute a new story to his vampire collection *The Midnight People*. The result was " Doctor Porthos ", which forms the basis of the next chapter of this book.

THIRTEEN

Doctor Porthos

As I have just indicated, one of the most difficult tasks facing an author in the field of the macabre today is investing old themes with new life. There are no new themes; that goes without saying. All the main classical strands: the ghost story, the tale of supernatural terror, cruelty, the monster, the vampire, the werewolf, and the two or three other variations on these basic plots have long ago been pre-empted by the masters of the genre.

What remains for the modern practitioner, particularly in the short-story field, is novelty of treatment. The atmosphere, of course, must be carefully sketched in, whether the story be half a dozen pages long or of novella-length. Similarly, the incidents should spring naturally from the story and while the tale must preferably shock and surprise the reader it should, above all, seem on reflection in all its incidents and plot-turns, inevitable.

This is a tall order by any account and one of the major reasons why so many of the macabre stories being written today fail to succeed and why there are so few masters in the field. One of the greatest, and perhaps the only legitimate successor to Edgar Allan Poe in the twentieth century, H. P. Lovecraft observed in his brilliant and classic essay, " Supernatural Horror in Literature "

The oldest and strongest emotion of mankind is fear, and the oldest and strongest kind of fear is fear of the unknown. These facts few psychologists will dispute and their admitted truth must establish for all time the genuineness and dignity of the weirdly horrible tale as a literary form.

Against it are discharged all the shafts of a materialistic sophistication which clings to frequently felt emotions and external events, and of a naïvely insipid idealism which deprecates the aesthetic motive and calls for a didactic literature to " uplift " the reader toward a suitable degree of smirking optimism.

But in spite of all this opposition the weird tale has survived, developed and attained remarkable heights of perfection; founded as it is on a profound and elementary principle whose appeal, if not always universal, must necessarily be poignant and permanent to minds of the requisite sensitiveness.

And he later adds in this long and highly perceptive exploration of the form: " With this foundation, no one need wonder at the existence of a literature of cosmic fear. It has always existed, and always will exist; and no better evidence of its tenacious vigour can be cited than the impulse which now and then drives writers of totally opposite leanings to try their hands at it in isolated tales, as if to discharge from their minds certain phantasmal shapes which would otherwise haunt them."

This is a truism which has seldom been better put. The short story, as we have seen, is a difficult form, and the short story of the weird, particularly of vampirism, is of a technical and artistic difficulty which need not be laboured. Stoker and Dracula cast a great shadow across the whole genre within the genre, i.e. the theme of vampirism within macabre literature as a whole.

The only method left is novelty of technique and surprise; in other words the writer should seek first to disguise that the theme is vampirism or that either the theme or the agency responsible for the vampiric happenings of the plot remain hidden until the end of the story. As I have pointed out in the last two chapters many of the novelists and short story writers of the late nineteenth and twentieth centuries succeeded brilliantly in their objectives.

With the same basic problems facing me I had yet another to contend with in writing one of my own most successful stories, " Doctor Porthos "—that of length. For technical reasons and the length of the commissioned book I was limited to a bare two thousand words. This partly dictated the diary form in which the story is cast, and, to make the incidents more vivid and immediate, I chose the first person, my hero being the husband of a young girl who is apparently wasting away from some form of pernicious anaemia. The story is cast in a deliberately Gothic mould. It begins as follows:

Nervous debility, the doctor says. And yet Angelina has never been ill in her life. Nervous debility! Something far more powerful is involved here; I am left wondering if I should not call in specialist advice. Yet we are so remote and Dr. Porthos is well spoken of by the local people. Why on earth did we ever come to this house? Angelina was perfectly well until then. It is extraordinary to think that two months can have wrought such a change in my wife.

The narrator of the story has been left an old house by his uncle, a mysterious recluse and the terms of his will state that to claim an annuity the couple must live there for a period of five years. Dr. Porthos meets the unnamed narrator at an inn near the mansion and from the first the young man distrusts him. The reader is deliberately left with the feeling that the doctor is something more than he appears: something sinister and sly, an impression which is reinforced by the narration which describes him as being " a tall, spare man, with square pince-nez which sat firmly on his thin nose ". He tells the nephew that his uncle died " of a lacking of richness in the blood ".

On arrival at the worm-eaten house the young man is dismayed to find that it is damp, being surrounded by a moat and that his uncle is interred in the old family burial ground adjoining the courtyard of the mansion. A week after arrival the young wife Angelina finds her health beginning to deteriorate. The husband calls in Dr. Porthos and then begins a sinister duel between them. The wife is apparently molested one night by a creature which pierces her throat; the husband distrusts Porthos and is frightened to sleep lest his wife should be attacked again.

The story arrives at its climax with both doctor and narrator mutually suspicious. So far, due to the first person narrative, all the vampiric atmosphere has surrounded Dr. Porthos; it is he the young man suspects; it is he who is discovered at the bedside late at night administering something to the wife.

In the final paragraph there is a complete reversal, when it is seen that the narrator himself is the vampire and that the doctor had been trying to save the wife instead of destroying her. The story ends:

Later. I awoke to pain and cold. I am lying on earth. Something slippery trickles over my hand. I open my eyes. I draw my hand across my mouth. It comes away scarlet. I can see more clearly now. Angelina is here too. She looks terrified but somehow sad and composed. She is holding the arm of Dr. Porthos.

He is poised above me, his face looking satanic in the dim light of the crypt beneath the house. He whirls a mallet while shriek after shriek disturbs the silence of this place. Dear Christ, the stake is against MY BREAST!

This last is, of course, artistic licence, because no one would be able to make a diary entry concerning their own dissolution, but the device is a perfectly legitimate one and works well in the context. How well was emphasised by Peter Haining himself in his printed commentary, when he observed: " With this tale the author again affirms that he is one of the most promising and inventive horror story writers to emerge in Britain in recent years."

Necessarily the vampire theme is one which the practising writer will not want to use more than once or twice in a lifetime and, indeed, why should he when there are so many other, equally fascinating themes from which to choose.

One exception to this rule I have previously mentioned. My old friend and publisher August Derleth was not only biographer, poet, essayist, regional novelist, a master of the pastiche in his Holmesian Solar Pons stories, critic, editor, film-script writer and many other things besides, but a uniquely gifted master of the macabre in the short-story form.

As befitted a man who was a giant in both physique and industry, with nearly two hundred books to his credit, he was also the author of hundreds of short stories. Many of them were in the macabre field and among that vast output were quite a number of outstanding tales of vampirism. I have already referred to one or two in the previous chapter. Since that was written, however, the world of letters has suffered a grievous loss with the untimely death of August Derleth at the age of 62 in July 1971.

It will not seem out of place, therefore, if I add an afterword here on a gifted master of the macabre—and in many other fields —whose loss will only be felt the more deeply as the years go by. He wrote to me shortly before his death to list his own vampire stories but, typically, could not remember them all. He first appeared professionally in print when he was 15 and said of this: " Indeed, my very first published story, ' Bat's Belfry ', was a vampire tale!"

Other fine stories in this genre included " The Satin Mask " and " Who Shall I Say is Calling?". Even more horrifying is " The

Tod Browning's 1931 classic film *Dracula*. Dracula (Bela Lugosi) is fascinated by the blood accidentally spilled by his guest, Jonathan Harker (Dwight Frye)

Count Dracula and one of his acolytes at Castle Dracula

The modern film Dracula, Christopher Lee, in a scene from *Dracula has Risen from the Grave* (1970)

Tenant ", which is worth some comment. A more subtle manifestation than is usual in vampiric tales, this is a terrifying
narrative of a horror, all the more telling for not being properly
glimpsed, which reaches out from a swamp to claim a living being.
As with many of Derleth's finer pieces, it first appeared in the
thirties and though widely anthologised, is rather more hard to
find nowadays. The scene is set, unusually for this writer, not in
the witch-haunted New England countryside which Lovecraft and
Derleth made peculiarly their own but in a kindly, sunlit England
and, more particularly, in an old country house surrounded by a
garden of some age and charm. Here, the protagonist Gerald
Paxton has come to see his old friend Sanbury. The house had
been left to Sanbury by his grandfather, who disappeared when
the former was quite young. Sanbury is particularly proud of the
rock garden which he and his hired man Jenkins, have made into
a showpiece. But Jenkins is a nuisance with his stories of an unseen tenant.

Subtly, as in most of Derleth's best stories in this genre, the
scene is laid, the beauty of Sanbury's garden contrasting bleakly
with the action of the story. The grandfather, Sanbury tells his
guest had an ugly reputation in the neighbourhood. It was said
that he used to abduct children as he needed living things to feed
his pet. The tension is beautifully sustained by this most subtle of
authors, working at the peak of his powers.

The other ingredients are a cellar which is smaller than it
should be and the discovery of a secret chamber with a slimy
bottom of black, deep mud. The story ends with shocking sud-
denness; there are slopping noises in the night and the thing—
which, as in the best tales of this kind, is never seen—ingests the
handyman in true vampiric style and goes back into its pit of
slime.

Says Paxton to his host. " My God! The tenant got Jenkins! "

Vintage horror, from one of the true masters of the twentieth
century, which brings to a fitting conclusion our examination of
the vampire theme in the short story. It is time to turn to the
treatment of the vampire on stage and in the cinema.

In Film and Theatre

FOURTEEN

Dracula on Stage

WITH THE popularity of Bram Stoker's horrific creation well assured before the turn of the century, it was inevitable with the opening of a new age, the advances made in stagecraft and technique and the rapid progress of the cinema, that new ways should be found of presenting the Count to an ever-widening public. With many populations still semi-literate, there was a vast audience to be captured and to whom the printed page remained literally a closed book.

More than two decades were to pass before *Dracula* as a living piece of theatre was evolved. It might perhaps have been expected that the New World, which was so forward in change and innovation, would have been first to produce the author of a stage version of the story and the success of the Hungarian actor, Bela Lugosi, in the New York production has somewhat overshadowed the British origins of the piece.

It fell to Stoker's old friend, Hamilton Deane, who was the son of the author's childhood companion, to adapt the story for the stage. Unfortunately, Stoker himself did not live to see it performed; his vivid creation treading the boards of a London theatre would surely have warmly appealed to his flamboyant personality, but in the event it was over a decade before the Deane dramatisation of *Dracula* was produced in London. Predictably, it was a phenomenal success, a number of productions were mounted over the ensuing years and the piece was still being performed during the Second World War by various touring companies.

The first stage production of *Dracula* the world had ever seen opened at Wimbledon in March, 1925 and it is interesting to note that two personalities who are still very much before the public were involved in this historic presentation. The part of Count Dracula was entrusted to a man who is now known as a distinguished stage, film and television actor but who was then a young and comparatively inexperienced player of 22.

Raymond Huntley, despite his youth, was an impressive figure as the Count and his performance could hardly have needed the artificial boost intended by the presence of a hospital nurse in the audience to go to the aid of those members of the public who succumbed to the horror of the play!

As always, the critics were less than rapturous, but the audiences, as is often the way, ignored their strictures and flocked to see the machinations of the wicked Count brought vividly to life by Huntley and an excellent cast.

Mr. Huntley kindly recalled his impressions of that long-ago production and in a letter to the author commented, " Hamilton Deane was an actor-manager who toured the provinces with a repertoire of plays; his version of *Dracula* was added to the repertoire and played up and down the country for some years. The play was brought to London and played there by Deane's touring company. Thus, it was not in the real sense a West End production."

The version of the play used in the United States and in which Lugosi appeared with such conspicuous success, was by John Balderston, and Mr. Huntley prefers the latter. He says:

Balderston's version was, I think, a better-made play; it was produced, directed and cast in a much more metropolitan style. My own connection with the play arose from the fact that as a very young actor, aged 22, I was getting some acting experience by playing in Deane's repertory company. Dracula was one of the parts I played and I came to London with the production.

I was invited to play it in New York but was unable to accept the offer and the part was played there by Lugosi. After the New York run I was again approached by the American management and played the part with the New York company on a national tour. You will understand from my point of view the whole thing was really just a part of my early training and experience; a youthful indiscretion perhaps!

Be that as it may and Mr. Huntley is certainly far too modest here, many people recall the production with affection and certainly the performances were invested with a suitably demoniac quality which made the stage version of *Dracula* a perennial favourite on a world-wide scale for nearly two decades. Raymond Huntley left the London production after a few months, in search of further experience.

He concludes, " My impression remains that the play had much more success in New York and the United States than it found in this country. The outstanding performance in both countries, I would say, was that of an actor named Bernard Jukes—since dead—who played the fly-eating lunatic."

Another well-known personality who was to become familiar to millions through television more than three decades later, was active in the stage production of *Dracula* both off and on the stage.

He was Jack Howarth, who was not only Hamilton Deane's stage manager in those days but appeared in this first version of *Dracula* as the Warden. He is very much better known in modern times as Albert Tatlock in Granada Television's long-running serial, " Coronation Street "!

So popular was *Dracula* as a stage play that it was successfully revived at London's Little Theatre in February, 1927.

The cast is worth noting. Raymond Huntley was supported by the author, Hamilton Deane as Abraham van Helsing; Stuart Lomath as Dr. Seward; Bernard Guest as Jonathan Harker; Peter Jackson as Lord Godalming; Bernard Jukes as Renfield; Jack Howarth as The Warden; Dora Mary Patrick as Mina Harker; and with Frieda Hearn, Hilda Macleod and Betty Murgatroyd in smaller supporting parts.

Hamilton Deane, the play's author, was the grandson of Colonel Deane, who lived on an adjoining estate to Bram Stoker's father, the Reverend Abraham Stoker in County Dublin for many years and he had great understanding of and affection for Bram Stoker's book. Nevertheless Raymond Huntley's opinion of the American play as the better piece is soundly based and Balderston's more sophisticated adaptation formed a solid groundwork for *Dracula*'s success in America and its later—and seemingly interminable—translations to the screen.

The London stage production later transferred to the Duke of York's Theatre, then to the " Prince of Wales " and finally to the " Garrick ". In all its venues it played to packed houses, as much a tribute to the fascinating formula evolved by Stoker in his book as to the undoubted skill of the players.

Hutchinsons, the modern publishers of one of Stoker's collections of macabre stories which appeared in 1966, recall an amusing incident during the play's long run. In a note to Stoker's collection, *Dracula's Guest*, they say, " This collection of stories by .Bram Stoker was first published in 1914. Later, a special edition of 1,000 numbered copies was issued for souvenir presentation to the audience at the Prince of Wales Theatre, London, on the occasion of the 250th London performance of the play *Dracula*—on 14 September 1927. When each member of the audience opened his or her mystery packet, he found not only a copy of *Dracula's Guest* but also, inside the book's cover, a black bat, powered by elastic, which flew out as the book was opened."

Unfortunately, Mr. Huntley has no recollection of bats flying high that evening but it must have been an impressive moment for London theatregoers and lovers of the macabre.

Dracula, as a stage play, went on gaining momentum and toured the English provinces with conspicuous success. Balderston's American version of *Dracula* opened at the Shubert Theatre, New Haven, Connecticut, on 19 September 1927. Another phenomenal run had begun and with it the opening of a sensational world career for Bela Lugosi, an actor whose name will be mentioned much in these pages.

Lugosi's film performances will be analysed in detail in later chapters, but his success in the New York stage version of the play gave Stoker's *Dracula* an impetus and a persona from which it was to benefit enormously. Certainly, the actor and the part were happily matched, and Lugosi, a Hungarian, whose tall, powerful figure and heavy accent seemed perfectly suited to Stoker's prose description of the Count, was to go on playing Dracula, in various media, for the next thirty years or so.

The New York cast of the play, which opened there in October 1928, was headed by Lugosi in the title role; with Terence Neil as Jonathan Harker. Another excellent impression was created by Edward Van Sloan as van Helsing, who gave Lugosi strong support. Van Sloan was to repeat the performance with marked success in the cinema, when he again appeared with Lugosi in the 1931 screen version. Raymond Huntley has already commented on the powerful impression made by Bernard Jukes as Renfield and this actor, repeating his original London stage performance, stiffened what was perhaps the strongest cast of Dracula the world stage was ever to see.

For the moment only those who paid to attend the theatre were being made aware of the power of *Dracula*, but the horror the character was to evoke at that time hardly sent a ripple through the wider world. Millions were to shudder over the next few years as Dracula finally rooted its fantastic success in the first screen classics based on Stoker's creation. One actor only—the unique Bela Lugosi—was to find immortality of the kind that the vampire of legend alone had achieved.

FIFTEEN

Nosferatu: F. W. Murnau and German "Decadence"

In 1922 came the first serious attempt to depict the vampire theme in the cinema. It originated, typically enough, from the German silent film industry which was pre-occupied, in the aftermath of the First World War, with escapist themes, fantasies and fairy tales, which emerged in an unparalleled flow from the brilliance of *The Cabinet of Dr. Caligari* in 1919 through the next decade with *The Nibelungenlied, Waxworks* and *Metropolis* on the way, ending only with the coming of sound in 1929.

Sound killed the German fantasy film and though there were attempts to re-create the genre during the sound period, the poetry and atmosphere eluded the film-makers, though paradoxically the Americans, whose silent horror films were mostly poor imitations of the Germans, created the best sound films in this style, including the definitive version of *Dracula*.

It fell to F. W. Murnau, destined to die tragically in a Hollywood motor accident at the height of his fame, to create the first essay in screen vampirism. His film *Nosferatu*, a generic Eastern European term for vampire, has been attacked, notably by modern cinema critics, for being " decadent ". The notion is an absurd one; as well criticise a musical for being light and frothy. Murnau's sombre tale, admirably photographed by Fritz Arno Wagner and Gunther Krampf, two outstanding technicians, responsible for much astonishing effects work during the " golden period " of

German silent cinema, is one of the primal source films for horror enthusiasts, and particularly for those interested in the legend of the vampire.

Based only loosely on Stoker's tale, Henrik Galeen's screenplay nevertheless follows the story-line remarkably closely, the locales being transferred to well-known German towns and villages. The Count, one of the great horror creations, is played by Max Schreck, whose identity has been the subject of much speculation among film historians. As *schreck* is German for fright, the artiste concerned, completely hidden behind grotesque and revolting makeup, was believed to have adopted a nom-de-plume. Whether this is so or not, the present writer has been unable to discover, but as the name Max Schreck also appears in listings of one or two other German silent films of the same period, there may well have been an actor of that name; this view is reinforced by some authorities who refer to him as a music-hall artiste.

Like Lugosi in the sound film, the portrayer of the central role makes the film, and what horror there is emanates entirely from his sinister presence and from the reaction of the young hero to the menace he exudes within the ancient castle walls. The film is marred by unfortunate effects and by some poor acting from supporting players. Murnau decided to use single-frame techniques to portray the coach gliding along among the Carpathian foothills and also for certain of the Count's actions, notably his loading a dray with empty coffins.

Stoker in his book describes the Count as moving quickly and jerkily; while this is impressive in print, Murnau, in his anxiety to be faithful to his source, has created moments which almost destroy the film. For these speeded-up sequences are ludicrous in the extreme, being more reminiscent of Mack Sennett than Gothic horror and they invariably have a hilarious effect on a modern audience. Murnau would have done better with slow motion, which would have conveyed the atmosphere of nightmare and terror much more impressively.

Despite these lapses, there is much to admire, notably a sequence in negative form, more than a decade ahead of its time, with tree-branches etched in black and ghostly white landscapes. The film opens promisingly and develops quite slowly, with the estate agent's clerk being despatched to the Carpathian Mountains on business. Unfortunately, the actor who plays his employer, and who is in reality in league with the Count, grotesquely overacts in his laboured reactions to the situation and Murnau holds these scenes on much too long.

But the film grips once Johannes is on his way and his slow journey to the inn, the warnings of the villagers and the final approach to the castle—with the reservations mentioned above—are beautifully done and are among the finest achievements of what may be termed vampiric cinema.

The first appearance of the Count—long delayed, thus setting a much-imitated tradition—is effectively realised, the spare, bowed figure, in close-fitting skull-cap waiting motionless in the castle courtyard, outlined against an archway. The film originally was heavily tinted, with dark blue night effects, as was the custom for most productions of the period. Unfortunately, modern prints of *Nosferatu* are in black and white only and so all the special effects are lost, the entire film appearing to be played in broad daylight. This is particularly disastrous with the Count's appearance in Bremen, where his walking down the street with his empty coffin under his arm would have convulsed the good citizens; it appears to take place in the bright light of day, yet the streets are entirely empty. With the original tinting the scene would have made sense, the deserted streets being depicted at dead of night.

Murnau breaks all the rules in this film, though one suspects he was less interested in the legend of the vampire than in telling a good story in the most striking way possible. Vampires cast no shadows, yet the film abounds in them; in fact it is sub-titled " A Symphony of Shadows "; to have done away with them would have robbed Murnau, as an outstanding silent film director, of many of his most striking effects. Quite rightly, he ignored this tradition. More questionable is his disregard of mirrors; as we have seen, the vampire returns no reflection in the glass, yet in the film we see the Count's reflection on a number of occasions.

These points will inevitably offend the purist, but as already noted, the director was probably concerned to present Schreck's performance in the most striking visual manner possible, without regard to detailed veracity. There are three great moments in this film, which make up for all its blemishes of style, presentation and acting. The first comes when Johannes descends into the castle cellar one morning in search of his host; peering through a crack in the lid of a great coffin in the vault, he is suddenly confronted with a huge close-up of the vampire in his trance-like sleep. The sudden visual shock of this is followed by the hero's equally rapid reaction in flinging back the coffin lid. This is treated in two separate shots and is an impressive demonstration of the power of the silent cinema to suggest noise—in this case, the cavernous clatter of the falling lid—and with the sound, the terror.

The second sequence is one where the heroine Lucy, who has determined to sacrifice herself in order to revenge herself on the vampire for the death of Johannes—unlike modern heroes, he succumbs to the attack of the monster—prepares to receive him in her room. She looks from her window and Murnau harrows us with a series of static shots in which the Count is standing balefully at his window looking across at the heroine. He then moves with infinite slowness out of the frame until we are left gazing at the empty window. Murnau knows the value of slowness in depicting terror—who has not felt the agony of slow movement in the grip of nightmare?—and with this sequence he brings the technique to high art. Which makes his insensitive use of fast motion earlier the more inexplicable.

The third great moment comes at cockcrow when the Count, surprised at his ghastly task, lifts his hideous face from Lucy's throat and stares at the window where the first feeble rays of light, that will soon dissolve him to dust, are appearing upon the sill. The sequence is an extremely fine one and as I indicated earlier, is one of three moments for which the film alone would be notable.

I have analysed these sequences in some detail, as they show an unusual grasp of the medium and 1922 was comparatively early for such sophisticated techniques. The print of *Nosferatu* in my collection is, unfortunately, a condensed version of Murnau's conception, but it contains all the best material. Max Schreck—pseudonym or not—has created a genuine original which transcends much of the primitiveness of the material, and has surely earned himself an honourable place in film history and in the history of the vampire.

SIXTEEN

"Children of the Night; Listen to them Howl!"

(Bela Lugosi as Count Dracula)

THE CINEMA seemed to have forgotten the vampire as a potent-
ially rich source of screen material. No doubt Murnau's film was
little shown in the wider world of America and the Northern
hemisphere, though it was much praised among the more
sophisticated in Europe. The fact remains that for almost a whole
decade after *Nosferatu* there was little or no attempt to illustrate
the vampiric theme through the powerful medium of film.

Then in 1931 appeared a production which drastically altered
the face of the cinema of horror and eventually launched a wave
of vampiric and other macabre beings on to the world, the forerunner of productions which show no signs of flagging forty
years after.

The name of the film was, of course, *Dracula*, and it brought
two personalities to world prominence. I will deal with Bela
Lugosi's career at some length in a moment, but the output of
Tod Browning (1882-1962), the creator of the 1931 *Dracula* is
worth more than a passing glance. Browning, perhaps more than
any other director, with the possible exception of James Whale
and Carl Dreyer, knew the importance of subtlety in depicting
the macabre. By 1931 he had already made his mark in the silent
cinema of the weird, notably with the Lon Chaney—Victor Mc-
Laglen vehicle, *The Unholy Three* (1925), which specialised in
shadows, the use of a fair background—which was to reappear in

his sound Grand Guignol essay, *Freaks*—and the hinting at of horrors too dreadful to depict openly. The method was to reach its apotheosis in *Dracula* and was to continue in a long and striking series of sound films in which Tod Browning left a small but distinguished reputation in the specialised genre of the horror movie.

Browning and his associates at Universal had the good sense to leave most of Bram Stoker's original tale intact. Even the introduction to *Dracula* is striking; instead of the thunderous music which was to become the hallmark of the horror film, *Dracula* begins with only the thin wail of a violin above the credits. A violin, moreover, whose scratchy, spidery melody conveys far more disturbing elements than a hundred-piece orchestra could have done. It is a small point but one typical of Browning's muted approach, which puts him among the masters of vampiric cinema.

The opening of the production could hardly be bettered; the Count's lair, the dank, malodorous vaults, with the camera panning slowly past the melancholy scene, alert at the slightest sound or movement; bones protruding from a shattered coffin; a rat gnawing listlessly at them; a spider scuttling into a corner and the freezing of the whole scene as the hollow noise of wood upon wood sounds through the crypt. Then the camera, with infinite slowness, begins its circling again—Dreyer was a master at this—until we see the source of the sound. The coffin lid lifts, a hand gropes, Dracula finally appears. The whole thing is finely achieved, typical of the film as a whole. Browning's *Dracula*, together with Dreyer's *Vampyr*, is a triumph of *mise-en-scene*. Mist, shadows, muted sound, darkness, night; of these elements are the poetry and atmosphere of horror truly built. There are few such works in the history of the cinema of the macabre and they stand as solitary sentinels in a vast landscape of mediocrity. As such they bear repeated study.

Bela Lugosi, whose work as Count Dracula in this film was to have such a striking effect on an international scale, was a former Hungarian cavalry officer, who had drifted to Hollywood after small parts in German and other European films. He was no great actor but in his earlier days was a commanding figure, with his smooth face, broad brow, jet-black hair and piercing eyes. This, coupled with a certain integrity in his acting, and his heavy, broken accent, made his Dracula a key-figure in the cinema of horror; it was a performance he was to repeat, with variations, in a career in films which lasted for something like thirty years.

That Lugosi himself recognised the uniqueness of his creation there can be no doubt; as we have seen, he had originally played the part, most successfully, on the stage in America from 1927 onwards and continued the Dracula role, with diminishing authority, until the ultimate degradation of the fifties, with the indifferent British comedy-thriller *Old Mother Riley Meets The Vampire*, in which he played second fiddle to the lugubrious Arthur Lucan. It would, perhaps, be kinder to pass over this aspect of his career. *Dracula* was a peak which he never again attained, though his reputation is safe for all time with this one performance.

Lugosi appeared in more than a hundred films, many of them of first-class quality—notably *The Black Cat* with Karloff, and an early American version of *Murders in the Rue Morgue*, but his Dracula is the key role by which he will be best remembered. We will, in a moment, consider the film as a whole, but first a few words more on Lugosi the man.

He was an artist who specialised in the darkness of the macabre and in the end the darkness reached out to claim him; in later years his own life was as horrifying as some of his celluloid creations. Drink and drugs broke a once powerful physique and he appeared in court in America in the fifties, pleading pathetically to be taken into hospital care. After increasingly soporific performances in cheap horror productions, in many of which he seemed to be sleep-walking, he was finally found dead in his apartment by a friend in 1956. Despite his abuse of a powerful constitution, he was then 72. That he had not forgotten the great days when the name of Stoker's creation was synonymous with his own, was evident from his will. In it, he directed that he should be buried in the scarlet-lined cloak he had worn as Count Dracula in Browning's film. His instructions were obeyed.

Browning's *Dracula*, as we have seen, showed the powerful effect a serious approach to the vampiric could have on mass audiences. This, coupled with acting of integrity, impressive art work and the intelligent use of sound and atmosphere proved that the theme, though inherently distasteful to the person of average intelligence and sensibility, could thrill without becoming repulsive. This was an artistic approach which might well have been noted by those who followed.

The smiling vampire, John George Haigh, on his way
to Brixton Prison on 11th March 1949

Highgate Cemetery, the haunt of vampire hunters

Browning and Lugosi went further. They not only remained reasonably true to Stoker's book, but they put in all the details of the legend with which the story of the vampire is surrounded so that the film may now be regarded, forty years on, as a sort of encyclopaedia of vampirism. Here is the spreading of garlic and wolfbay to keep the creature from the sleeper's chamber; the recoiling from the crucifix; the lack of reflection in the mirror; the thirst for blood which can even be slaked by eating flies or other insects, failing a human victim; a terrifying shot of the Count descending the castle wall head first, like a great bat; the wolf running across the lawn—which, however is more germane to lycanthropy than true vampirism—and, finally, all the paraphernalia of the disposal of the dreaded creature; the sharpened stake and the final dissolution of the monster, implied rather than crudely visually stated.

All these excellences—striking though they were—would not be enough without Lugosi's Dracula, a commanding if malign figure, and excellent support from the supporting cast. Some latter-day critics have denigrated the film for implied staginess and certain failings among the small-part players; while this may be true to a certain extent it is well to remember that any work of art should be considered in its context and time. The film is quite unashamedly based on a stage play and thus is bound by certain conventions—it was scripted by Garrett Fort after the stage presentations by Hamilton Deane and Balderston—but its general merit is not vitiated by its stage origins; rather it gains from them and much of its treatment, especially of the exteriors, is highly cinematic.

Witness the arrival of Jonathan Harker at Dracula's castle; the meeting in the Borgopass at midnight, the hooded coachman with his glowing eyes, the nightmare journey of the coach which makes no sound as it lurches across the rough terrain, the howling of wolves in the distance above the wind, and the giant bat which hovers over the leading horse's head. This is the horror film *par excellence*, the *stimmung* of the Germanic Gothic film re-created in an American studio, and a unique example of vampiric terror.

Dwight Frye, who scored in a number of horror films in the early thirties, notably as the dwarf in the first two *Frankenstein* films—in fact in all five of the Universal series in various roles, made a first-rate Jonathan Harker, the catalyst through which the vampiric influence operated. His early scenes with Lugosi's Count in the mouldering old castle are some of the best in the film; such as the shot where he has to cut his way through festoons of cobwebs with his walking stick up a staircase down which the Count has just passed with ease and without breaking the web. The fine atmospheric photography was by Karl Freund.

Memorable too is the dinner-table sequence where Lugosi tells him with grim emphasis, " I don't drink—wine." Browning is particularly good in the scenes in the madhouse where the inmate is invoking the name of his invisible master and trying to obtain sustenance for his terrible needs by catching flies and other insects. These are images of terror which stay in the mind for years and have seldom been bettered.

Edward Van Sloan's Professor van Helsing was a solid creation too and set the pattern for Cushing's performances thirty years later.

As in most of the vampire films to follow—with the notable exception of Sybille Schmitz in Dreyer's *Vampyr*—the women are disappointing, the Mina and Lucy of Frances Dade and Helen Chandler never really rising to their opportunities, though the bevy of female vampires who advance on Harker across the misty terrace in an early scene form a beautiful image with the imposing figure of Lugosi's Count suddenly appearing to order them back from his chosen victim.

Above all, the film enchants today for its very lack of emphasis on the things which in modern cinema would be insisted on. It has the striking black and white photography by the great Karl Freund; a fine reticence in rigidly eschewing crude horrors; a subtlety of playing and presentation in certain scenes which chill by Browning's careful selection of detail; the power of Lugosi's playing, already noted; its use of mist, shadows and stillness; and the patina which age seems to give to the images of these old films and which cannot be recaptured by the razor-sharp focus and depth of modern photographic techniques.

Browning's *Dracula*, together with Lugosi's magisterial performance as—dare one say it—the noble Count, will surely be revered by connoisseurs of the genre as long as celluloid can be made to hold together.

SEVENTEEN

Terror in the Mist: Carl Dreyer's Vampyr

THE WORLD is full of mist. Through the blinding whiteness mysterious figures move, slowly and enigmatically, like drowned persons. There are strange noises whose causes cannot often be traced. Fantastic shadows gyrate to the jerky music of a polka on a vast wall. One dies and is screwed into one's coffin. Shadows of trees brush the glass lid as one is carried gravewards. An old woman, the cause of this living death, peers downwards into the coffin.

These brief fragments are not extracts from some surrealist manifesto, though they might well be. Nor are they sections of a script for Antonioni or Resnais. The time is 1932 and the images are from one of the most remarkable films ever made. The film was *Vampyr* and the director the Dane, Carl Theodore Dreyer, one of the most profound minds ever to be connected with the cinema.

I use the terms remarkable and profound deliberately, because *Vampyr* is unlike any other film on the theme ever made before or since. Its treatment and subject are refreshingly different; the adaptation is from Sheridan Le Fanu's *In a Glass Darkly*, instead of the over-familiar Stoker; the centre of evil is an old woman instead of a man; the whole conception, direction and playing is at least thirty years ahead of its time; and, above all, by its images and style it creates a powerful impression on the spectator.

Indeed, unlike Browning's *Dracula*, which Dreyer may have seen and admired, *Vampyr*'s originality went largely unnoticed at the time, and, like the ripples emanating from a stone thrown into a pool, its reputation has slowly grown over the last forty years, until it occupies a pre-eminent position in the cinema of terror. There are people who have been to see *Vampyr* ten, fifteen, twenty times, wherever and whenever it is shown, such is the magic its extraordinary atmosphere exudes. For *Vampyr* is a true original and there is no film quite like it, either in the field of the macabre, or in the more conventional paths of cinema.

When Dreyer came to make *Vampyr*, a year after the world-wide success of the film version of *Dracula*, he was already the internationally acclaimed director of a great classic of the silent cinema, *The Passion of Joan of Arc*, in which the actress Falconetti, aided by the cameraman Rudolf Maté had laboured to produce some of the noblest images the silent cinema had ever seen. His profoundly moving works in the sound cinema, such as *Day of Wrath* need not concern us here, but Dreyer undoubtedly had an imagination drawn to the strange borderlands of the mind and much of his work is witch-haunted.

Day of Wrath itself, is a tremendous symphony of terror, with its witch-hunt and searing finale; St. Joan is haunted by dreams and visions, of course, and many of his modern-dress films have passages of strange fantasy.

One of Dreyer's earliest films, *Leaves from Satan's Book*, directly inspired by Griffith's *Intolerance*, chronicled the evil exploits of the devil through the ages. In a much later, short sound film called *They Caught the Ferry*, made in 1948, Dreyer painted a horrifying picture of a young couple on a motor-cycle, racing to catch a ferry across to one of the Danish islands, who are lured on to disaster by an old man driving a ramshackle car which, however, they are unable to overtake. The old man, in a *Nosferatu*-like make-up, turns out to be Death and the ferry the couple eventually catch is Charon's boat which slowly pushes out across the Styx.

The frightening authority of Dreyer's style—and he is one of the world's greatest film directors—made the images of *Vampyr* bear far more weight than would be possible in the normal type of horror film and therefore this production is worth studying at some length.

Dreyer was born in Copenhagen in 1889 and after a brief career as a clerk gave up his job for journalism, became a balloon pilot, and then started writing dialogue for Nordisk Films. He graduated to film direction with *The President* in 1918, and so, when he came to make *Vampyr*, had a long and distinguished list of films, including at least one masterpiece, behind him in almost fourteen years of active film direction.

The story of how *Vampyr*—also known as *The Strange Adventures of David Gray*, came to be made and the history of its production, is extremely interesting in itself and is related at length by the distinguished Danish film critic Ebbe Neergaard in his monograph on Carl Dreyer, which appeared in this country under the British Film Institute's imprint in 1950, and to which I am indebted for a number of details in this study.

But I cannot agree with some of Neergaard's conclusions on *Vampyr*, the theme of which he feels did not interest Dreyer a great deal. A close study of the film itself reveals many strange insights into the nature of vampirism, which gives it its peculiar power. Like *The Cabinet of Dr. Caligari*—to which, however, it bears no physical resemblance at all—it seems to contain an inner core of evil which pulses out of the images and literally harasses the spectator.

Dreyer was lucky in two things on this film: he had broken away from his employers and was able to finance a relatively inexpensive production in France through the young Baron Nicolas de Gunzburg, a wealthy dilettante and art-lover, who backed the film and played the title role of David Gray under the stage name of Julian West.

Despite attacks by some critics I find his performance in the film not only interesting but satisfying, and though he is not called on to display any profound emotions, he is an effective catalyst through which most of the ghostly emanations in the film come about.

It was Dreyer's good fortune to again have with him one of the world's finest cameramen, Rudolf Maté, who had already evolved the austere images for *Joan of Arc* and was to make an incredible contribution to *Vampyr*, as will be seen. Unfortunately, the world lost a great director of photography, when Maté forsook the camera to become a Hollywood director.

Though some of his films, such as *Miracle in the Rain*, were extremely interesting, one still feels his greatest contribution to the development of cinema—particularly in the macabre and fantastic field—could have been behind the lens.

There is not much of Le Fanu in *Vampyr* and, as we have already seen, *In a Glass Darkly* was not a story at all, but the generic title of a collection of stories. The derivation of *Vampyr* is our old friend, " Carmilla ", of course, though little remains of the original but the general theme and a few details. However, this matters not at all in Dreyer's hands, for a literal screen adaptation of " Carmilla " would have resulted in nothing more than a Scandinavian " Brides of Dracula " and with Dreyer's eventual creation we have an undoubted masterpiece.

There is a minimal story and what there is remains confusing and vague—deliberately so, in the manner with which Resnais and Antonioni particularly have today made us so familiar. The whole film is based on *stimmung*, and Dreyer proved in *Vampyr* that a great work of vampiric horror could be sustained on atmosphere alone. Much of the credit for this must go to Maté's contribution on the photographic side.

The incident is well known; shooting had commenced but Dreyer was not satisfied with the material he was getting; none of the effects he was after were being realised. One day he drove past a plaster-works in his search for locations and the white dust which coated everything gave him the idea of having the evil doctor in the film choked to death by flour in one of the steel mill cages. This sequence became the key for the film's style. Maté experimented and found that black gauze placed over the camera lens caused a light diffraction, giving the film the misty, overall tone which was to make it unique in film history. The Baron was in complete agreement and the enthusiastic film-makers proceeded to shoot the whole picture using the method.

What is the story of *Vampyr?* It can be told quite briefly. David Gray (de Gunzburg) arrives at a small country inn where enigmatic things happen; he passes a sinister form in the corridor; he witnesses a strange *danse macabre* of shadows on the wall of a château, cut to the jerky rhythm of a polka. He is given a package by a stranger who visits his room and later finds it belongs to the château owner, one of whose daughters is attacked by an obscure, wasting illness.

After the Count is suddenly shot, David Gray opens the parcel and discovers a volume on vampirism. How film-makers love this detail! It occurs in scores of lesser films and forms a key sequence in *Nosferatu*, where Gustav von Wangenheim, the Johannes/Jonathan Harker of the story finds a similar book in his room.

The vampire herself is a departure for the genre, resembling a cinematic equivalent of Benson's " Mrs. Amworth ". For she is a gentle old lady, whose misty images have a particular quality of terror, belied by her appearance.

She was played by an amateur, the widow of a French factory owner, and in fact there was only one professional in the cast. The vampire is assisted in her work by the sinister village doctor, in whom Dreyer saw some demoniac quality which had gone unnoticed by his friends and colleagues in real life.

Later in the film David Gray has an appalling dream, which is one of the great sequences of vampiric cinema. He dies and is screwed down in a glass-lidded coffin, through which the old vampire woman peers at him. Towards the end of *Vampyr*, David Gray and one of the château's servants seek out the vampire's coffin and drive a stake through her heart in the traditional manner. The scene is cross-cut with a shot of the daughter, Leone, being released from her bondage to the vampire and returning to normality. The film has tremendous style and will bear repeated viewings.

Ivan Butler, in his interesting study *The Horror Film* makes the sapient point regarding *Vampyr* that whiteness is one of the results of loss of blood and that Dreyer makes full use of it in his essay on vampirism. The simile is extremely apt and sums up the essence of this strange film. There are many bravura moments which stand out. The most distinguished is undoubtedly the coffin-dream; the effect on the spectator is claustrophobic as the lid is screwed down on to Maté's staring camera-eye and we, the audience, are left looking at the trees blowing in the wind as we are carried gravewards in striking tracking shots by the coffin bearers.

One of the most menacing static images in cinema is the shot where the old woman is discovered in the open air, bent over her victim on a bench by a lake, in the cold pre-dawn light. A basically commonplace camera set-up is given horrific content by Maté's extraordinary camera technique and the shimmering quality of the mist which surrounds vampire and victim. This is macabre, and revealing and at the same time ordinary, an effect which is not often achieved in any medium, let alone the cinema.

The death of the doctor in the ice factory and the polka have already been mentioned. The contribution of Sybille Schmitz, the only professional actress in the picture, a graduate from Max Reinhardt's acting school in Berlin, gave the film a disturbing tension in two scenes. One is where her love for her sister changes into vampiric blood-lust—she had previously been attacked by the old woman—and the other is in the finale in which she is released from bondage. As other writers have observed, these key close-ups could only have been achieved by a professional actress and they heighten the effect of terror which Dreyer maintains throughout.

There remains then the mist which gives the entire film its atmosphere and remoteness; and the cunning use of sound, which frets at the nerves, as "noises off" are heard but never quite located by the camera.

Dreyer died in the mid-sixties, well into his seventies and having continued filming—albeit at long intervals—almost to the end of his life. Except for the short subject, They Caught the Ferry, noted earlier, he never again ventured into the realm of the macabre. This was a great loss to the genre as the true film masterpieces on the vampire theme can be counted on the fingers of one hand.

That the subject of vampirism proved a worthy one for minds of the calibre of Dreyer, Murnau and Browning must be counted fortunate. In the case of the Dane, it seems fairly safe to say that Vampyr will remain a unique masterpiece that will not be duplicated in our time. If Dreyer had made this production and no other, his reputation would still be safe.

EIGHTEEN

Dracula Lives Again

FOLLOWING THE inimitable performance Lugosi gave in *Dracula* it was perhaps inevitable that his talents should be utilised in sequels until, as usually happens, degeneration set in. The films became increasingly shoddy, passing beyond the ken of Universal; whole shoals of imitations sprang up until the genre died of exhaustion some time after the Second World War, only to be revived in the late fifties by the British firm of Hammer Films, who—whatever reservations one may have of their content—certainly created a major commercial success, the company's shares today being quoted on the London Stock Exchange.

Dracula's Daughter (1936) was one of the best of the sequels, being modelled on the excellent fragment Stoker excluded from the main framework of *Dracula*, and which was later published as the short story " Dracula's Guest ". It would be tedious to detail the innumerable re-makes of the theme in B-picture terms, but a trend may be marked here and there and some of the more noteworthy versions indicated. Even Lon Chaney senior had played a vampire in the silent *London after Midnight* in 1927, but the effect was ludicrous pantomine.

Dracula's Daughter had perhaps the most distinguished cast of the re-makes, with the master himself re-creating the dignified Count, heading a line-up which included such notabilities as Otto Kruger, Irving Pichel, Edward van Sloan once more, Nan Grey, Hedda Hopper, Claude Allister, E. E. Clive, Halliwell Hobbes and Billy Bevan.

Robert Siodmak, who had collaborated with Billy Wilder and

others later to become famous on the celebrated German documentary *People on Sunday* in the thirties, himself directed *Son of Dracula* in 1943, with a cast headed by Lon Chaney; but a Dracula film without Bela Lugosi was rather like Hamlet without the Prince and the film remained generally undistinguished, despite occasionally impressive effects. There were some half-dozen or so attempts to inject life into the film cycle of vampirism between the mid-thirties and the mid-forties, and these sporadic efforts, feeble though they generally were, eventually unleashed the flood-gates of the genre, culminating in the Hammer horror cycle, lasting more than a decade and at the time of writing showing no sign of flagging; while the Italian cinema through the sixties ground out cheap vampire pictures which, however laughable, reaped impressive figures at the box office.

In the late fifties the American cycle finally petered out. In 1957 Universal-International produced the mediocre *Blood of Dracula*, known in England as *Blood is my Heritage*, with a cast of completely unknown and largely forgettable actors. With its final gasp, however, the American industry generated a momentary flicker of interest in 1958 with United Artists' *Return of Dracula*.

Though cheaply made, this production, known in England, for some obscure reason as *The Fantastic Disappearing Man*, starred the once-great Francis Lederer. Lederer, originally known as Franz Lederer, appeared in such notable German silent films as Hans Schwartz's *The Wonderful Lie* and Pabst's *Pandora's Box*, in which he gave superlative performances. With the rise of Nazism he went to America and created an impact in 1941 in *Confessions of a Nazi Spy* with Edward G. Robinson and some years later played opposite Paulette Goddard in Renoir's Hollywood-made *Diary of a Chambermaid*.

Though saddled with such intractable material as *The Fantastic Disappearing Man*, it was predictable that so distinguished an actor should make something of the role of Dracula. The film made the fatal error of placing the character in the modern urban setting of America with Lederer as Bellac, a man who, like the mysterious stranger played by Joseph Cotten in Hitchcock's *Shadow of a Doubt*, comes to stay with relatives in a small town. He is the heroine's cousin and even she is puzzled at his penchant for lying in bed all day and his nocturnal sorties.

Perhaps the best moments occur early on when a female vampire appears in the dark foliage across the railway tracks of a lonely country railway station and beckons to the solitary passenger on the platform. This is an imaginative sequence and includes, as do so many of the films, the legend of the werewolf; as we have seen, Browning's *Dracula* employed the verbal " image " of a wolf running across the lawn, and the same device is used here, though again we are only told of the appearance, not shown it.

Despite the general shoddiness of the production Lederer's anguished performance is an occasionally disturbing one and at least his vampire comes to an original end: pushed by accident into a pit in a struggle with the heroine, to become impaled on a stake. The production went out on second run in British cinemas in the early sixties and was revived on commercial television in mid-1969 during a late-night horror cycle. Its title was a complete misnomer, though the original may have been changed to avoid confusion with Lugosi's 1944 *Return of the Vampire* from Columbia, in which he was co-starred with a better-than-average cast, including Nina Foch, Frieda Inescourt and Miles Mander.

While dealing with the vampire theme in B pictures it is not without significance to note that many otherwise distinguished actors made " guest appearances " as Count Dracula and in almost every instance were absolute failures. In fairness it must be added that the films themselves were almost complete parodies, such as *Abbott and Costello Meet Frankenstein*: even Lugosi, who appeared as " himself " in the foregoing, was hard put to it to make any impression amid the welter of slapstick and among a cast which included Chaney Junior, Lenore Aubert and Glenn Strange.

However, a classic example of the genre run to seed comes in *House of Frankenstein* (Universal, 1944), a sort of Hellzapoppin of monsterland, in which Bela Lugosi plays Frankenstein's monster, Lon Chaney Junior the Wolf Man and John Carradine Count Dracula! All three men were responsible for distinguished work in their time, Carradine particularly so and the film is all the more incomprehensible in that the cast also includes such 100-carat artistes as Patrick Knowles, Ilona Massey, Lionel Atwill, Maria Ouspenskaya and Dwight Frye, who created such an excellent impression in the original *Dracula*.

Carradine just cannot get to grips with the part, such as it is. A mad light glinting in his eye and with his top hat and opera cloak at rakish angles he looks more like J. Worthington Foulfellow in Walt Disney's *Pinocchio* than the wicked Count! Commercial television were extremely unwise to end with this production as the last of five *Frankenstein* films screened in mid-1969 in Great Britain.

An ingenious by-product of the vampire theme utilised the talent of Bela Lugosi to greater advantage in two films which are worth consideration. The first of these was *The Vampire Bat*, directed by Frank Strayer for Majestic Productions in 1933; It had a lavish cast headed by Lionel Atwill, Fay Wray, Melvyn Douglas, George E. Stone, Dwight Frye and Lionel Belmore. Even more interesting was *The Devil Bat*, produced in America in the late forties.

Though the latter unfortunately suffered from cheap B picture production methods and some insipid supporting players, the best of whom was Dave O'Brien, the film had an interesting central performance by Lugosi. He played Dr. Paul Carruthers, who suffered from the delusion that he had been cheated of enormous profits by a gigantic American cosmetics company. He accomplishes his revenge by training a giant bat to kill on scenting a particular perfume.

He selects his victims—all partners in the company—by presenting them with gifts of a new type of shaving lotion which contains the killer perfume. The idea is a novel one and, though the picture suffers from lack of the really expensive photographic techniques which would have made it outstanding, the scenes of the bat diving on its victims are quite excitingly handled, and *The Devil Bat* is today an engaging and unusual essay in the vampire genre and exceedingly rare. Lugosi meets his end, as may be imagined, when the hero himself throws some of the perfume on the doctor's clothing and he is then attacked and killed by the bat on its return to the laboratory.

Roman Polanski, the brilliant Polish director of macabre subjects, possibly said the last word on screen vampirism with *The Dance of the Vampires* (1967). The key scene comes with the vampire selecting his male victim and setting to work. The victim, with rare spirit, bites him instead and the vampire goes screaming with rage and indignation round the balcony of his castle!

Perhaps, with the whole range having been covered, from the growth of the genre with *Nosferatu*, through *Dracula* and its host of imitators plus the Italian pot-boilers—which are for the most part not worth the listing, though *Black Sunday* (1961) with the inimitable Barbara Steele is a brilliant exception—it was time, more than two decades afterwards, for a more serious and solid approach. The modern revival was, strangely enough, to be a completely British enterprise.

Hammer Films, a modest studio, with headquarters at Bray on the Thames, hit the jackpot in the mid-fifties when they launched into the series of horror productions which made the company the biggest and most consistent money-spinner in the British industry. Now, more than a decade and over a hundred films later there seems no slackening in the output.

The beginning of their success, it will be no surprise to learn, was *Dracula*, directed by Terence Fisher in 1958, based closely on Bram Stoker's original. Fisher became the foremost exponent of the vampire theme in the modern cinema and may have directed more productions on the Dracula myth than any other man in film history. A dubious distinction, some might think, when much of Hammer's footage is devoted to the sadistic, not to say sickening detail.

But on the credit side there is much to commend the films: solid playing from an experienced and talented " stock company " of distinguished actors, headed by Christopher Lee and Peter Cushing; first-class photography; opulent décor; the use of colour, which gives the Count's scarlet cloak—not to mention the blood!—an added impact and, above all, a continuity in playing and style. Apart from Universal Studios in Hollywood, this was what the American excursions into the genre lacked. One would think that audiences would become satiated with such a limited visual theme, but as fresh generations grow up, the demand for the films seems to increase rather than slacken. At the time of writing Hammer Films are confidently preparing their programme for the next decade.

Along with the umpteenth sequel to *Frankenstein* and the *Wolf Man* that we shall be seeing in 1980, will be yet more stories about Bram Stoker's deathless creation. The company can have had little inkling of the perennial popularity of the theme when they approved Jimmy Sangster's original screenplay for the pilot film, *Dracula*, in 1958. Though Sangster toned down the supernatural element of the Count's character, thereby eliminating such striking visual effects as the Count climbing vertical walls over frightening chasms, what we got in the persona of Christopher Lee was a commanding authority in the playing; a demoniac presence, combined with Mr. Lee's physical stature and a sort of controlled ferocity in the presentation, which audiences evidently found physically frightening.

Christopher Lee's Count Dracula is hardly subtle in the Lugosi tradition and he certainly does not replace the Hungarian in the pantheon of great screen creations, but his bloodshot eyes (even more effective in colour) and particularly his agonies in disintegration—the Hammer productions are chillingly expert on this aspect—give him a vivid, if flashy edge, on his predecessors.

He is finely aided in the illusion by the authoritative playing of Peter Cushing, who appears in most of the Dracula films in the old van Helsing part and invests it with something of the authority of Sherlock Holmes, another literary character which Cushing has played with conspicuous success, both on the large screen for Hammer and in a British television series. Most of the Hammer *Dracula* productions contain certain felicities of detail and almost all are stuffed with first-rate British character actors, which gives them a great advantage over their American counterparts, which usually have to make do with the scrapings of the back-lot to pad out their casts.

Some of the effects are very fine; a notable moment in the first Hammer *Dracula* comes when Cushing approaches the Count's castle just in time to see a driverless hearse, its galloping horses with nodding black plumes rapidly bearing its melancholy load along the lonely country lane. All the more pity then that the films are infested with often nauseating close-ups of the blood-stained eyeball variety and the company even specialises in additional revolting inserts which are exported to such countries as Japan, where they apparently enjoy such delicacies.

When the Hammer vampirism is good it is very good indeed; if the company had combined the first-rate photography and acting with the sensitive atmosphere of the best of the American and German films on the same subject, they would have created masterpieces which would still have been box-office successes.

Fisher's second film, *Brides of Dracula*, was possibly the best, though without the benefit of Christopher Lee; I will pass over it now as I deal with it a little later. The third piece, in 1965, *Dracula—Prince of Darkness*, also handled by Fisher, had some beautiful settings and some great moments of terror but was ruined for me by a sequence reminiscent of a butcher's shop in which Dracula's ashes were rescuscitated in a veritable bloodbath. The sequence was as unnecessary as it was ludicrously re-volting. It is rather strange, too, that no one has yet realised the idiocy of re-creating evening dress, tie, cape, top-hat and cuff-links from the basic ingredients of blood and ashes.

For sheer atmosphere, one of the later Hammers', *Kiss of Evil* would be hard to beat. The whole film is based on the building of tension and the milieu of the vampiric family, who infest the Transylvanian village above which their castle stands, is superbly sketched in. The production opens impressively with the pre-credit sequence of a funeral service in the village's Gothic grave-yard, horrifyingly interrupted by the Professor of Clifford Evans, who shatters the coffin-lid with a spade; the scream which follows and the blood which oozes from the lid are almost as startling to the spectator as to the mourners.

The way in which the honeymoon couple, with their Edwardian motor car, are drawn into the web spun by the family of vampires is subtly done; the settings are sumptuous and impressive; and one of the highlights is a masked ball in which the dancers move to the excellent mood-music created by John Hollingsworth, while their grotesque masks leer soul-lessly at the spectator.

The finale of the film is a fine amalgam of black magic and vampirism, with the sinister villain, excellently played by Noel Willman, surrounded by his white-robed acolytes willing the heroine-victim to come to him, while Clifford Evans works at a pentacle to bring the forces of evil to destroy the vampire-nest in the castle. In one of the most original climaxes in horror cinema, an army of vampire-bats smash their way through the stained-glass windows and bury Willman and his followers be-neath their palpitating wings. Highly satisfying Grand Guignol and one for the specialist.

There have been several more *Dracula* films since, all with the same essentials of the earlier films, most marred by the same unpleasant details. All the more pleasing, therefore, to be able to recommend another of the series whole-heartedly, in a production Tod Browning or James Whale would not have been ashamed of.

A film which stands out from Hammer Films' standard *oeuvre* is *Brides of Dracula* (1959) directed by Terence Fisher with style and finesse. It is not without loose ends but has the advantage of opulent décor and distinctive performances from the distinguished and experienced cast of veteran players. More attention is paid to detail and the build-up of .the film is impressive, as it should be if the uncanny is to succeed in the cinema.

The prologue sees a young woman travelling through Transylvania in the person of Yvonne Monlaur, who gives a fresh and attractive performance in the role of potential victim who is always saved at the last moment. Lee does not appear in the production—after all, as the opening commentary says, the monarch of the Vampires is dead!—but he is hardly missed when the vampire-countess of the late Martita Hunt is on screen.

Miss Hunt has given many outstanding performances in a long career but she was seldom better than in this weird and compelling appearance, reminiscent of a Sheridan Le Fanu novel. A secondary mystery which gives the film added distinction is heralded by the chained apparition of a handsomely blond young man, played by David Peel, who appeals to the girl to release him from the bondage of the sinister countess. The heroine is singularly obtuse even for Transylvanian legend, and when the young man is released she takes several reels to realise that her erstwhile fiancé is not only the Countess's son but has been chained up because of his vampiric tendencies.

The story is further strengthened by the father figure of Peter Cushing in the central role of the girl's saviour, van Helsing; he seldom puts a foot wrong in the murky sub-plots which follow and he and Miss Hunt carry the film between them, though there are other rich plums for the connoisseur. There is an absence of cliché in that the vampiric centre of evil is not a sinister and dark figure muffled in a cloak but a Byronically handsome young man, whose metamorphosis is all the more shocking when it comes. The mist rises as thickly as ever, it is true, and the vampires—both male and female—have a tendency to grow instant fangs, never visible in the remainder of their time on the screen, but let those details pass.

Brides of Dracula is Hammer at its considerable best and a bevy of talented character actors give memorable vignettes. There is an extraordinary moment, which teeters dangerously towards pantomime, when the old gypsy serving woman, played with wild gusto by Freda Jackson, lies on the grave of Miss Monlaur's newly buried girl-friend Andrée Melly and croons, " Push, my precious! "

For the specialist too there are nicely calculated performances by Henry Oscar as the snobbish and mercenary principal of a private school and by the greatly underrated Mona Washbourne as his equally genteel wife. Much-needed light relief is provided by the incomparable Miles Malleson as a bumbling village doctor who assists Professor Cushing in his diagnoses.

Despite its many improbabilities and occasional infelicities of dialogue, *Brides of Dracula* is a triumph of décor and solid acting expertise, while the central performances of Martita Hunt, Cushing and Peel, prove once again the compelling fascination of the vampiric theme in the cinema of terror.

In Fact

NINETEEN

Medical Vampirism

FROM THE vampire of the cinema and theatre, with his smoulder-
ing eyes, black cloak, masterful manner and flamboyant adventures, is a far cry to medical vampirism. We turn now to the dark
pages of factual history and the colours grow increasingly sombre
with every tortuous step we take. By the term medical vampirism,
I do not necessarily mean a vampire in the supernatural sphere,
but a being whose morbid and unnatural thirst for human blood
must be slaked by living victims—or even by the recently
dead.

Necessarily, this is a field almost as fiendish and cruel as the
vampire proper and the sadistic monsters to be met with in these
pages, such as Fritz Haarman and Haigh, run their fictional
counterparts very close. Indeed, some would say—and who would
argue with them—that the monsters of reality are far more
frightful than those of legend and fiction and it is a sobering and
terrifying reflection to realise that the last of them met his well-
deserved end only three decades or so ago.

And who knows what similar crimes in trim suburban streets
may go unrecorded? Certainly, the number of times some of these
criminals struck and went unrecognised and unpunished, must
give any thinking person pause. Many of these monsters claimed
a fantastic number of victims before the authorities acted, and
even in the mid-twentieth century only the foolish actions of one
of the most notorious brought his dreadful crimes to light; and
by then, the death-toll may have risen to as many as nine.

What then, is a vampire in the medical sense? it may be asked. For the purposes of this book, I am excluding such practices as those indulged in by remote African tribes, whereby their members, at initiation ceremonies, lick blood from knives used to cut themselves and others; and also the disgusting practices of Mau Mau and some secret societies in which blood features in rites and ceremonies. As interesting as some of these might be, I feel they are properly excluded here, not only on grounds of length.

To my mind, a vampire in the true medical sense, is a person who by reason of powers beyond his control must have human blood to quench his unnatural thirst; he first obtains suitable victims whom he renders powerless and then attacks; either killing them in the process of drawing blood or, even more horrible to most people, obtaining the nourishment he needs after the victim is dead. This is not a pleasant subject, of course, but it must be dealt with if the present volume is to attempt to be reasonably comprehensive in scope.

Here we will necessarily be dealing with criminal matters, though the trials and other judicial proceedings in which the human vampires were brought to justice, will only be lightly touched on. Again, greed for money or possessions of the victims, will hardly enter into the reasoning of the true vampire, although many of the cases dealt with, include persons—one can hardly call them human—whose motive was partly gain, coupled with the lust for blood. What do doctors themselves say about this fortunately rare disease? I call it disease for want of a better term, but the craving for blood is obviously unnatural and the method used to obtain that blood in the case of human beings, must of necessity be criminal and depraved.

The medical men involved in the cases I have examined all agreed that true cases of medical vampirism in man are rare, so rare in fact, that only one genuine case has been recorded in England this century. When we come to the nineteenth century and earlier periods, then records are sketchier and one must obviously tread with care when hearsay is involved. Though the details of these cases are horrific and sordid, no thorough study of vampirism should be without them and certainly, the interesting and gripping incidents involved in these instances of medical vampirism give strong backing to the material of the legends.

As we have seen earlier it is extraordinary what a wealth of vampiric legend emanated from the blood-soaked earth of the Eastern European kingdoms from the earliest times and down through the Middle Ages. It is not quite clear why this should be so, but the history of the eastern states of Europe has been particularly bloody, with larger nations fighting over possession of the smaller, so that the reality could almost be said to have provided the sadistic patterns for the legends.

One who seemed to be in the true vampire tradition was the horrifying Countess Elizabeth Bathory, who gained the reputation for vampirism in the sixteenth century and actually lived in Hungary, classic ground for the ravages of the undead. Said to be a necrophilist as well as a sadist, the Countess was reputed to be a sort of vampire queen. Stories which have come down to modern times claim that she murdered several hundred young girls and drank their blood, but there is, of course, nothing tangible which we should regard in the twentieth century as evidence of these horrors.

The Countess, who was born in 1560, was brought to trial in 1611 after the authorities had raided her castle during an orgy. Girls were found tortured, and chained in dungeons and apparently used as living cows, being " milked " of their blood as needed. The Countess's blood-lust was said to have been aroused when she scratched her maid with a comb in a fit of temper and found blood on her hands. She had the impression it did her skin good and actually bathed in it.

Her accomplices in crime were beheaded but she, being a noblewoman, was imprisoned in her own castle. The authorities formally condemned her to life imprisonment and she was walled up in her own bedroom. She died four years later on 25 August 1614. Hammer Films made an interesting and rather distinguished film on her life in 1970, somewhat predictably called *Countess Dracula**. Mercifully, she seems to have had few followers in a sombre field she made peculiarly her own.

---

* *Countess Dracula* was directed for Hammer Films in 1970 by Peter Sasdy, a brilliant young Hungarian who fled from his native country during the uprising and became a television director in England. Sumptuously mounted and photographed in Eastmancolor, *Countess Dracula* was fairly faithful to historical fact and had an excellent cast, with Ingrid Pitt as the Countess, supported by Nigel Green, Peter Jeffrey, Maurice Denham and Sandor Eles. I mention it here because it has an unusual and ingenious plot not at all germane to the normal " vampire " film, despite its title, and therefore lies outside the scope of films discussed in Hammer's Dracula series earlier in the book.

If the stories told about the Countess—or even a tenth of them—were true, she would be a vampire in the medical sense, who used her privileges of *droit de seigneur* in the same way as many of her contemporaries—for vice, lust, perversions and all manner of abominations. She would seem to be in the tradition of a similar monster, Gilles de Rais, who suffered from haematomania, to give it its true medical term. This is literally a lust for blood, and certainly the whole of de Rais's life was tinged by this madness, just as his countryman de Sade was obsessed by sex and sexual cruelty. De Rais was a fifteenth-century pervert who was a Marshal of France and fought alongside Joan of Arc in her campaigns against the English. The Black Baron was executed in 1440 when it was alleged he murdered a large number of boys and girls in a human sacrifice to the Devil.

In his classic fiction study, *La Bas*, Joris Karl Huysmans refers to de Rais as a vampire, though he could not be so described in the supernatural sense. Rather was he a maniacal sadist and necrophilist whose blood-lust was a by-product of his cruelty. One of his most infamous acts was said to be that of sitting in the bowels of a living boy while drinking his blood. If it is not too cynical a view de Rais and his noble friends who gathered at his château in France, passed their time in the traditional manner for people of their century and class: that is with whoring, wining and dining, orgies and pederasty.

Certainly, from the records which have come down to us, things occasionally got out of hand, but it is difficult to take some of the statements about de Rais seriously. Like all such " records ", they should be scrutinised with a degree of scepticism, but nevertheless de Rais must be ranked among medical vampires. One of his more pleasurable pursuits concerned the dismemberment of children. Like many men before and after him, he had a penchant for small boys, but in his case they were enticed to his château, outraged, tortured and then dissected piece by piece.

Gloating in the middle of this holocaust de Rais would drink the boys' blood as fancy took him. His vampirism would then be satisfied for a time. Some of the descriptions of this nobleman's activities are too revolting, even for a study of this sort, but de Rais, who has received a number of full-length studies could in no way be considered a " vampire " in the main tradition, as his lust for blood was apparently connected with sexual activity, a not uncommon symptom in medical case-histories over the centuries.

As a super-sadist he was almost unique; as a vampire he was in the minor league.

There are many stories throughout history, purporting to deal with authenticated cases of vampirism; some of them we have dealt with in earlier chapters when discussing the legends of this most frightful of all fiends. But the truly genuine record of the activities of the medical vampire is hard to come by; of necessity it is blessedly rare; proper records of such matters as to render the case even for the sceptic beyond dispute were not kept until comparatively recent times; and, of course, many instances have been hushed up or buried anonymously in the pages of medical journals of an earlier age.

The dreadful ravages wrought in Scotland in the fifteenth century by Sawney Bean, the Edinburgh peasant who issued from a remote cave with his band to literally devour lone travellers, has sometimes been cited as a case of vampirism. Considered properly, Sawney Bean's activities and those of his clan of fifteen—eight sons and six daughters were included—are a clear-cut example of cannibalism, and for this reason I have reluctantly excluded this famous family of monsters from the present study. Bean and his family were executed at Edinburgh in 1435, but the echoes of their terrible atrocities still vibrate a high, shrill nerve of horror in the sensitive of our own day.

In the eighteenth century Eastern Europe and Hungary in particular seemed to be favoured by the activities of the vampire. Dr. Herbert Mayo, a well-known Victorian surgeon, who once practised at the Middlesex Hospital, published a popular work on superstition in mid-century, in which he devoted some space to vampirism in the eighteenth century. Of this period he says, " Vampyrism spread like a pestilence through Servia and Wallachia, causing numerous deaths and disturbing all the land with fear of the mysterious visitation, against which no one felt himself secure."

He cites as fact a case of vampirism in Belgrade in 1732, in which many people in that city were attacked, as though by a malady and sickened and died. The military, as often happened in earlier times, were appealed to by the citizenry and took a hand in laying the monster. Dr. Mayo dealt in detail with the medical symptoms of the vampire's victims, as might be expected; laying stress on the anaemia and haemoplegia which followed the attacks. He says that the military authorities eventually opened the grave of the vampire in one of the city's cemeteries, when the skin of the corpse was found to be fresh and ruddy and the mouth running with blood from the thing's feast of the night before. The military, who included as witnesses three surgeons and a Lieutenant Colonel, dealt with the monster promptly and in the time-honoured manner. A stake was driven through the chest of the creature " which uttered a terrible screech while blood poured in quantities from the wound ". The corpse was then consumed by fire and presumably the district was troubled with the terrible scourge no more.

Authentic outbreaks of vampirism in America are comparatively rare and have been little recorded, possibly because the United States has a shorter history and records consequently cover a comparatively brief period in time. In 1874 in the small community of Placedale, Rhode Island, a Mr. William Rose himself dug up the body of his own daughter. He then burned her heart, apparently in the literal belief that she was exhausting the vitality of the remaining members of her family. The occurrence was recorded in a newspaper of the period and if true sheds a curious light on this corner of a then rural America.

Miss Rose, according to her father, would have been a vampire in the true supernatural sense and in the matter of " exhausting the vitality " of her own family would have been behaving in exactly the same manner as the thing which attacked the hero of de Maupassant's classic short story " The Horla ", as we have seen in an earlier chapter.

Cases of vampirism in Ireland are equally rare, if records are to be believed. An interesting account of an authentic instance appeared in a journal at the turn of the century, which dealt with the occult. The events took place many years earlier, which places them within the framework of Victorian society and were related to the author of the article, a Mr. R. S. Breene. He says:

It was from Roman Catholics who described themselves as eyewitnesses that the information was derived. Again, I have read that vampirism only appears in countries which are in a backward condition as in some areas of Eastern Europe. The people amidst whom the events took place were Roman Catholics, yet they are not of a high type. The country is wild, isolated and mountainous. Even in recent years numerous terrible crimes of violence have been reported from the neighbourhood, some of them of a peculiarly senseless character. I was myself shown, some years ago, a spot marked with a white cross upon a stone by the roadside, where a lad of about twenty years of age had kicked his father's brains out, on no apparent provocation.

Breene goes on to relate the history of a local priest who was put in charge of a small hill parish in the Irish countryside of which he is speaking. He continues:

He was hospitable to strangers, and had frequently placed beds in his little parochial house at the disposal of belated travellers and even tramps. Yet no one in his immediate neighbourhood would have thought of going to see him socially. They went to him on the church's business or they did not go at all. He was, in a word, respected, though not greatly liked.

When he had little more than passed his fiftieth birthday he suddenly fell ill and died after a brief confinement to his chamber. He was buried with all the simple pomp that surrounds the obsequies of an Irish country priest. His body was removed before the funeral to his mother's house which was several miles distant from his parish. It was from there that the funeral took place; then the coffin set out once more from the white-washed farmhouse, to carry its occupant upon his last journey to the rocky graveyard in the hills where all his kin had laid their bones for generations. The bereaved mother was left to her thoughts for the rest of the day in the house of death.

Meanwhile the funeral cortège wended its slow way toward its destination in the mountains. They did not waste much time in getting their sad task over and done but they had a long road to traverse and the sun was already declining in the heavens as they climbed the last succession of hills on the way to the homestead they had left in the morning. Night was already in the air. The shadows were lengthening below the hill crests, but upon the white limestone highway, everything was still broad daylight.

At the foot of a slope the mourners in the first cars suddenly became aware of a solitary figure coming down towards them walking rapidly. As the distance between them and the pedestrian lessened they were surprised to see that he was a priest. They knew of no priest who would be there at such a time. Those who had taken part in the ceremony at the grave had not come so far with them on the return journey. They began to speculate as to who the man could be. Remarks were exchanged and meanwhile the newcomer had met the foremost car.

[Breene goes on,] Two men were awake in it. There could be no mistake. They saw at once and quite clearly, that they were face to face with the man whom they laid in his grave two or three hours before. He passed them with his head slightly averted, but not sufficiently to prevent them from making absolutely certain of his identity or from noting the intense, livid pallor of his skin; the hard glitter of his wide open eyes and the extraordinary length of his strong white teeth, from which the full red lips seemed to be writhed back until the gums showed themselves.

He was wearing not the grave clothes in which he had been attired for his burial, but the decent black frock and garments to match in which they had last seen him alive. He passed down the long line of vehicles and finally disappeared around the turn of the road. Someone in every loaded trap or car had seen him, particularly those who had been awake and on that side. A thrill of terror passed through the whole party. With hushed voices and blanched cheeks they pushed on quickly, now only anxious to get under some sheltering roof and around some blazing hearth before dread night should fall upon them.

Their first call was at the farmhouse of the dead man's mother. In the front was a little porch built around the door, a small narrow window on either side. About this they gathered and hurriedly decided to say no word of what had happened to the bereaved mother. Then someone knocked but received no answer. They knocked again and still being denied admittance, they began to be uneasy. At last someone thought of peeping in one of the little side windows, where he saw the old lady lying face downward on the floor. They hesitated no longer but literally broke in and it was some little time before they were able to bring her around again to consciousness. This, briefly, is what she told them.

About half an hour earlier she had heard footsteps on the flags outside, followed by a loud, challenging knock. She was surprised that they should have returned so soon and, besides, she had been expecting the sound of the cars approaching. She decided that it could not be any of the family and so, before opening, she looked out at the side. There to her horror, she saw her dead son standing in the broad daylight, much as she had last seen him alive. He was not looking directly at her.

[Breene concludes his extraordinary account by adding,] But she too, noted the extraordinary length of his teeth, the cold blaze of his eyes, the wolfishness of his whole bearing and the deathly pallor of his skin. Her first instinctive movement was to open the door. Then fear swept over her, swamping even her mother love. She felt her limbs giving way under her and quickly sank into the oblivion in which she lay until they found her.

There are many other such recorded stories of the eighteenth and nineteenth centuries but this seems to be one of the best and most vivid accounts of its kind I have come across, though it is one of the few recorded instances of a vampire appearing in daylight. Though apparently a supernatural appearance of a true vampire, I have included this account among the reports of medical vampirism for several reasons. The apparition was not seen again, it appeared in daylight and no one was attacked.

It was also unique in that a great number of people saw it, in the clear light of day and that it was a corroborated account which took place in fairly modern times. An example of mass hallucination, perhaps? Who can tell?

We enter the present century with a celebrated horror of the twenties which is often cited as a classic instance of vampirism. I do not think myself that this is so, but the crimes involved merit a description by reason of the manner of inflicting death; the murderer killed a number of boys by biting them in the throat, which earned him the nickname of " The Vampire Killer ". We shall consider the circumstances of Fritz Haarman in the next chapter.

TWENTY

Fritz Haarman: Horror in Hanover

HANOVER, A great railway town, in 1918, in common with most of Germany was in chaos; the centre for refugees, escapees from camps and detention centres, it was thronged with the human débris thrown up by the aftermath of the First World War. Its geographic and natural centre was the Bahnhof, the huge central railway station into which its floods of refugees ebbed and flowed with the movements of the timetables in endless tides of misery.

Among them, along with prostitutes, homosexuals, criminals and all the riff-raff dislodged from its natural habitat by war, were scores of homeless boys who had come to Hanover quite aimlessly, perhaps hoping for work, or more often merely to loiter at the centre of activity and to see what life would bring with the dawn of each new day. These huddled masses of all ages and classes would doss down for the night in halls, corridors and third-class waiting-rooms and the traveller became used to picking his way through this bundled flotsam on his way to and from the trains.

One person who habitually used the station had more than a passing interest in its itinerant refugee population. He was well-known to the Hanover police force, who did their best to keep an eye on the teeming hordes of refugees, but as might be imagined, their numbers were thin for this almost impossible task of sur-veillance. This man sometimes helped the police in keeping watch, and from midnight until early morning, he would patrol the platforms and waiting areas, occasionally questioning the young-

sters as to why they were there; where they had come from;
where they were going; or whether they had any relatives.

There was a method in these apparently aimless questions,
which had developed a pattern in their repetition over the years.
Very often a hungry and frightened boy would confide in this
burly and not unsympathetic man in his late thirties. The stranger
would listen in a kindly manner and when he had made up his
mind would offer the hospitality of a bed and a meal in his living
quarters at a cook shop he ran in the old quarter of Hanover.

Many of the boys who accepted the invitation of the kindly
stranger were never seen again. Their host, who was later to be
accused of no less than twenty-seven murders, was a man called
Fritz Haarman, a small-time criminal, pederast and police informer. He first held his victims down by hand before killing them
with one bite on the throat; it was this method of killing which
was to cause the newspapers of the day to dub him the " Hanover
Vampire " and to cause a thrill of horror to run round the world
when he was brought to trial in 1924.

Though Haarman cannot truly be called a real vampire, his
method of killing his victims bore all the classic hallmarks of a
vampire attack and the Gothic horror which surrounded the
crimes is worthy of some examination. Some of the facts of the
case were undoubtedly toned down by the authorities at the time;
though twenty-seven victims was the official count, it was un-
officially estimated that as many as fifty murders of young males
between the ages of 12 and 18 could be laid at his door in almost
five years of criminal activity, and horror was heaped upon horror
when the court proceedings revealed that he had added cannibalism to his crimes.

The prosecution alleged that he had actually sold the flesh of
his victims for human consumption in his cooked meat shop;
there was no doubt that Haarman had been able to outdo all the
local butchers in the reasonableness of his prices and it was observed that he had never been short of meat at a time when it was
particularly scarce during the aftermath of the war. He had once,
it was alleged, cooked sausages containing human meat and ate
them in his kitchen. One cannot help noting the resemblance of
the Haarman case to that of Sawney Bean, briefly mentioned
earlier. Even more striking is the parallel with Prest's popular
melodrama *Sweeney Todd*, whose demon barber sold the bodies of

his human victims to provide the ingredients of the pies sold in Widow Lovat's shop next door. A case of nature imitating art, perhaps? Or was it possible that Haarman, ill-educated and ignorant as he was, had made himself familiar with the old story?

The vampire's first victim was a boy of 17 called Friedel Rothe who disappeared in early October 1918. His parents, who had received a postcard from him, posted from Hanover a few days earlier, instituted a thorough search for their son and Haarman's home, Cellarstrasse 27, was raided by the police, who found Haarman in an extremely compromising position with another youth. He was arrested and sentenced to nine months' imprisonment for gross indecency; at the time of his arrest the head of the boy Rothe was hidden under a newspaper behind an oven in his home! Later, he threw the head into a canal. But for the lack of thoroughness in the police search of the meat shop, Haarman's vampiric activities would have come to an abrupt end and twenty-six lives have been saved.

Almost a year after his arrest, in September 1919, Haarman met a handsome youth called Hans Grans, who was to be his downfall. Grans was almost more decadent than the older man and is described by Montague Summers as " one of the foulest parasites on society ". Certainly he was a male prostitute, thief, informer and murderer, apart from having various sidelines such as blackmail and *agent provocateur*. He was responsible for many of the murders, urging Haarman to kill in one instance because he coveted a youth's shirt; he often acted as the decoy, bringing the hapless victim to the vampire's den. This is not too strong a term as the squalid circumstances of the murders involving Haarman and Grans were unspeakably sickening.

The court proved and the two men confessed that when they were in the cook shop premises, Haarman held his victims down and then murdered them, usually by a single strong bite on the throat. In many cases the victim's body was then cut up, sometimes being cooked and eaten in various forms by Haarman and Grans. Those portions of the bodies of the twenty-seven unfortunates not eaten by the vampire or his friend, were then cooked and sold to the public over the counter of the shop.

Another man, a butcher was also involved in disposing of the " meat " supplied by the infamous pair, but he seems to have been a minor figure compared to them. Haarman was trapped when a quarrel broke out between him and a potential victim at

Hanover Station in June 1924. Both men were arrested and the horror was revealed when Haarman's room in the aptly-named Red Row section of the city was searched. Haarman then implicated Grans in his crimes and the unholy couple stood trial in a case which was a *cause celebre* on a world scale.

The *News of the World* was only one of scores of newspapers which had a field day with the trial; a typical heading in large type was " Vampire's Victim ". Haarman's background was interesting, in view of cases we shall be examining at a later stage. He was the son of a railway-engine stoker and though dull and stupid seems to have made a good impression on the German Army, serving in Alsace with the 10th Jager Battalion. He had spent some time in an asylum after being convicted of offences against children and had an angry and quarrelsome relationship with his violent father, the two men often coming to blows. In 1903 he was medically examined with a view to his being sent to a home, but the doctor involved felt there were no grounds for returning him to an asylum. He became a tramp, street hawker and thief and later, at the time of his association with the Hanover police, was known as " Detective Haarman ", in view of his work as a police informer.

There does not seem to have been any tangible clue to the reason for his vampiric traits and his mental and moral disintegration seems to have been a gradual descent, aided by the general degradation of the company he kept and the complete collapse of all standards in Germany following the Great War.

When his methods of killing his victims in the fashion of a vampire and his eating of the remains were described in court, Haarman sat unmoved and impassive throughout the most horrific evidence. Most interesting though, was his denial of insanity; he protested that he was in a state of trance when he attacked his victims and did not realise what he was doing. But the prosecution argued tellingly that this could not be so as the method of killing, which involved holding the victim as he bit into his throat, argued premeditation of the crime.

The macabre details were increased when Haarman and Grans described the crimes, the bones and skulls of the murdered boys being thrown into the river, which abutted on to the vampire's quarters. The producers of a Grand Guignol film on this theme, could hardly improve on the horrendous circumstances of the crimes or the *mise-en-scene*. Though Haarman was undoubtedly a vampire of sorts, he seemed at the trial hardly to be the dominant partner; he alleged that Grans beat him for sometimes failing to bring down the "game" brought to him. Bodies were often stacked in a cupboard awaiting dismemberment and once the police were actually present when a victim's corpse was hidden only a few yards from them.

Hanover, and to some extent the world, breathed with relief when Haarman was decapitated by sword in April 1925. Surprisingly, his equally infamous companion Grans escaped with life imprisonment, later commuted to twelve years' penal servitude.

Montague Summers, who described the case in his book, *The Vampire: His Kith and Kin*, says of Haarman, "This is probably one of the most extraordinary cases of vampirism known. The violent eroticism, the fatal bite in the throat are typical of the vampire, and it was perhaps something more than mere coincidence that the mode of execution should be the severing of the head from the body, since this was one of the efficacious methods of destroying a vampire."

While we need not go all the way with this pronouncement, Summers's is an apt description of the Hanover Vampire and one can only agree, with a slight degree of qualification, when he adds, "Certainly, in the extended sense of the word, as it is now so commonly used, Fritz Haarman was a vampire in every particular."

Before we bring the sombre history of medical vampirism up to date by advancing further into the twentieth century we should now return for a while into the nineteenth; for a horror which rocked the civilised society of France and England. A series of classic crimes which in their setting and background might have come from the pen of the great Gothic writers of horror; once again nature surpassed the art of fiction in the circumstances surrounding the bizarre history of Sergeant Bertrand.

TWENTY-ONE

Sergeant Bertrand: the Phantom of Montparnasse

THE GATES of the cemetery were securely locked and had been since dusk. Though it was a summer's evening it was cold for the time of the year and thin wisps of mist undulated slowly among the gravestones. For the watchers it had been a long vigil and looked like being an even longer night. One of the guardians of Montparnasse eased a cramped muscle and the minute rustle his clothing made against the undergrowth brought a sharp hiss of reproval from the army officer at his side.

They were a strangely mixed company to be gathered together in a cemetery at this time of night and they were engaged upon an even stranger errand. The dim light glanced on the barrels of the rifles, while the dark butt of a pistol shimmered through the mist as the officer lowered his hand to consult a heavy silver watch he took from an inside pocket. It was past eleven; not ten minutes earlier the deep-toned bell of a neighbouring church had tolled the hour. Spread out across the cemetery, concealed behind the blanched bulks of monuments or screened by damp, funereal shrubbery were the grey-tunic'd soldiers from one of the Paris military garrisons.

Here and there among the smarter-dressed military were burly men in roughly-cut blue overalls: the guardians of the great cemetery who by day tended the walks, did a thousand small tasks for the dead and who closed and locked the ponderous gates of the sad city of ghosts each evening at dusk. Phlegmatic, unimaginative men, who had to be of necessity to carry out their trade, yet even they, usually insensitive to atmosphere, cast uneasy glances behind them from time to time, reassured by the weapons of the military and by a stiffening of seasoned sergeants and corporals among the more callow rank and file. The guardians carried pitchforks and clubs and other improvised weapons from their daily toil, though one or two of the more militant fingered muskets of an older, colonial pattern, which drew amused glances from the senior troop members.

It was difficult to realise that the greatest and fairest city in the world lay only a hundred yards beyond the thick belt of trees which sighed in the wind. Or that Montparnasse might again this night be visited by the phantom who had been seen so often over the past months, flitting through the city's graveyards and cemeteries, intent upon his grim and horrifying task. All Paris had been sickened by the reports, which indicated to a startled and sophisticated capital that, incredibly, a vampire was at work in metropolitan France.

It was the year 1849 in a century of extraordinary progress yet the activities of the fiend the troops were set to capture had instilled fear into thousands who had read for months in journals and bulletins the stories of his monstrous activities. " The Vampire ", as he was known throughout France and indeed in England and even farther afield had first appeared in Pere Lachaise, where some of the most illustrious in the arts of painting, music and literature were buried, earlier in the year.

The guardians of Pere Lachaise had been terrified to see a shadowy figure flitting among the tombs at dead of night, but it had an extraordinary knack of eluding its would-be captors so that men began to whisper that the night visitor was a supernatural being. Graves were found desecrated in the most shocking manner, bodies were torn from their coffins, violated and apallingly mutilated. Reports in the press were circumspect for that day and age, but there was evidence, the authorities said, that vampirism was involved.

The police and the civil authorities were unable to apprehend the monster and after a while the atrocities at Pere Lachaise ceased. All was quiet for some time and then the horror began again, this time in a Parisian suburb where a quiet cemetery containing the bodies of ordinary folk was the scene of violent and inexplicable events. The public was outraged when the body of a small girl of 7, who had been buried only the day before, was found torn from her coffin. Her corpse had been apallingly disfigured and mutilated. Once again police and military were moved in; a shadowy figure was glimpsed but as before the visits grew more sporadic and finally ceased.

Then, in midsummer the necrophilist began his horrifying work at Montparnasse Cemetery, where the exhumations and the vampiric attacks on the recently dead were on such a dreadful scale that the authorities were forced to take extra-special precautions. The view grew that the manifestations must be supernatural. This was strengthened by the fact that every cemetery which was the scene of the attacks was surrounded by high walls and guarded by heavy iron gates, which were always kept locked after nightfall.

Yet the phantom had made his escape on innumerable occasions, after scenes of the most frightful sadism, with such consummate ease that the supernatural theory grew, despite all the efforts of the authorities to keep the rumours within bounds. Small wonder that even seasoned troops moistened dry lips and grasped their carbines more firmly as the night wind whispered among the branches.

It was still a little short of midnight on this particular July evening when the captain in charge of the military was momentarily startled to have his arm grasped by one of the guardians at his side; he followed the trembling finger the man held out and was disturbed to see a dark figure gliding among the tombstones in the middle distance. Muttered orders went out along the line and the thin crescent of military and cemetery guardians began to close in. All was silent for a while and then the night air was disturbed by the hideous sound of ripping woodwork.

The captain was unable to control himself any longer; he jumped to his feet, arm upraised and barked a command. There was a moment's hiatus while the line of men got to their feet, then the unmistakable clatter of a coffin lid falling on to the gravel pathway. A figure, low and indistinct bounded away among the gravestones with incredible speed. The pallid ray of a dark lantern probed among the misty graves as several rifles barked out as one.

There was a moment's confusion, men rushing through the tombs, colliding with cold marble and each other. Then a terrible scream rang out in the darkened cemetery and with it several rifles gave tongue again, the bright flashes stabbing the charnel darkness of Montparnasse. The captain, a guardian panting at his side pounded up the gravel path. Something snarled, a figure bounded to the cemetery wall and was gone in the suddenly clamorous night. N.C.O.s conferred excitedly, there was a relieved jabber of noise; the captain called for the lantern.

By its yellow rays they saw dark splashes on the ground; the officer probed them diffidently with his finger. Blood! So the visitor was not supernatural, after all. They hurried to unlock the cemetery gates; there were scrapes as though made by boot marks on the wall. The trail of blood went on down the boulevard outside. The troops took up the chase in triumph. In this way the most notorious vampire of the nineteenth century, Sergeant Victor Bertrand, was followed and trapped.

The foregoing scene in Montparnasse Cemetery was of necessity a reconstruction. It was not, as might be imagined, a romantic episode from a Gothic novel as penned by a Prest or a Bram Stoker, though none loved such plots better. It was nevertheless a reconstruction based accurately on historical fact, and with these ingredients the sensation caused by the arrest of Sergeant Bertrand in mid-nineteenth century Paris can easily be imagined. For what writer would have concocted such a wealth of vampiric detail. The cemetery at night, the scene set in summer, instead of the wintry night of fiction writers; the military and the guardians waiting for a fiend who had already carried out unspeakable ravages in a number of suburban Paris cemeteries; the shadowy figure's approach; the ambush; the firing; the disappearance of the phantom; and above all—deliciously apposite—the vampire's own blood spilt and that in itself leaving a trail from which followed the monster's capture and arrest.

Today, with all the advantages and disadvantages of television and the other mass media, Sergeant Bertrand's case would have been known throughout the world within a single day. Even in the 1849 of limited communication, the case was to be a sensation for a decade and even within a very few weeks had gained wide European notoriety. For the vampiric predator had left not only blood behind him. The eager searchers, anxious to put an end to the horrors which had plagued Paris for months, came across some scraps of military uniform. The cemetery intruder had been severely wounded, as could be deduced from the colour and quantity of the blood and later that same evening a party of sappers of the 74th Regiment stationed in Paris said one of their sergeants had returned to barracks badly injured.

So serious were his wounds that he had been taken direct to the Val de Grace, the Paris military hospital, and within a short while of visiting the hospital the police realised they had got their man. When he was fit to be questioned Bertrand said he had an " irresistible impulse " to visit cemeteries, to disinter the corpses which he then violated; he was hardly conscious of what he was doing, as he fell into a form of trance after the attacks came on. The authorities found that the details of the mutilations of the corpses and the defendant's practices on them were of such a horrifying nature that much of the circumstances surrounding the crimes was suppressed.

But there can be little doubt that Bertrand, who was known throughout Europe as " Le Vampyr " was a necrophiliac and addicted to vampiric practices. As such and quite apart from any supernatural aspect, he was the direct forerunner of Stoker's super-monster, and the French public, by the thrill of horror which ran through their journals, was fully alive to the romantic and Gothic aspect generated by Bertrand's terrible deeds, to use the term romantic in its true and decadent sense.

This was fully borne out at the court hearing on 10 July 1849, when the Paris council of war proceedings, headed by a Colonel Manselon, were attended by vast crowds of people, among whom were many attractive ladies and others not so young. Not for many years had the city had such a *cause celebre* and both the public and the public prints made the most of it. Bertrand's evidence would seem to have been intended to convey the impression that he was of unsound mind.

Medical evidence, however, adjudged him sane and, as no murder was involved, the vampire-Sergeant was sentenced to a year's imprisonment and with that dropped out of sight and out of history. The word classic is overworked and perhaps is used rather frequently in these pages, but if ever the term were deserved surely it applies in full measure to Sergeant Bertrand, whose shadowy deeds in the darkness of nineteenth-century Paris made him the monster of Montparnasse.

TWENTY-TWO

The Crawley Crimes: John George Haigh

ONE BLEAK February day in 1949, in a country of ration cards and austerity following the greatest war in history, a middle-aged company director turned the key in the padlock of a warehouse he rented on the outskirts of Crawley, Sussex, and secured it for the night. The building was a brick, two-storey structure, with two small windows at the front, situated in an area known as Giles Yard. Surrounded by a 6-feet-high fence, the warehouse fronted Leopold Road on the outskirts of the Sussex town.

It was owned by a light-engineering firm known as Hurstlea Products Ltd., who used it for storing surplus materials, including steel beams, which could not be housed at the firm's main premises in the town itself. The warehouse had latterly been used by the director for experimental purposes known only to himself and at night it would have been an isolated enough spot for such activities, although there were other premises nearby. The building had a neglected air and was surrounded by the squalor of industrial débris, with an old water tank standing at one side of the main window and timber stacked against the outer wall at one end.

The man who so prosaically locked up the premises after his day's activities seemed the acme of respectability; dapper in his appearance, he was a typical businessman with his well-groomed hair, neat military-style moustache and plump, smooth face. He described himself as an engineer and for several years had been living in a quiet hotel in Kensington. A former choirboy and grammar-school pupil he had led a solitary childhood; the effect of two conflicting systems of religious thought had resulted in a strange dichotomy in his character which was to lead to his undoing. Unknown to the other guests in the hotel he had spent several periods in prison following various swindles in which he had been involved.

By the late 1940s he was in a difficult financial situation and his insatiable appetite for money, which he could well have earned honestly if he had applied his natural gifts in the right direction, had led him into a steeply spiralling downward path which culminated in circumstances of peculiar horror. Behind the door of the storeroom as he locked up for the night were the ingredients of crimes which were to make the director's name a household one throughout the world and to reveal him as a mercifully unique casebook of medical vampirism.

The items behind the locked door included two carboys of sulphuric acid, a revolver and documents. Round about the premises were scattered forms of sludge later found to contain human remains. The man so coolly leaving for London was later to tell the police that he had murdered no less than nine people; had drunk their blood after death; dissolved their bodies in sulphuric acid to remove all traces of the crimes; frequently drank his own urine and felt himself, on the evidence of his own words, to be completely above the law and the reach of human justice.

The man's name was John George Haigh, and the horror released among the public when the details of his atrocious behaviour were made known is perhaps unique in the annals of twentieth-century crime and also in the tangled byways of medical vampirism; here, if anywhere, was the classic example of a nineteenth-century vampire in twentieth-century surroundings.

The circumstances of Haigh's arrest and his being charged with murder—he was indicted for only the one crime—can be told quite briefly, as the general circumstances of his trial and subsequent conviction are beyond the compass of this book. In February 1949, Haigh, then aged about 40, though looking older, was living as a long-term guest at the Onslow Court Hotel in South Kensington. Also at the hotel, where she had been staying for about six years, was an elderly widow, a lady of 69, Mrs. Olive Durand-Deacon. She and Haigh were on the usual terms of friendly acquaintance common among hotel guests, but there was another woman in the hotel, a Mrs. Lane who had formed a close attachment to Mrs. Durand-Deacon. It was to Mrs. Lane that Haigh spoke on 18th February, when he mentioned that Mrs. Durand-Deacon was to have accompanied him to Sussex the day before but· had failed to meet him as arranged. It was in this manner—typically he could not resist making the first move— that Haigh prepared the way for his own destruction, additionally linking the missing woman with the Sussex area.

Haigh again asked Mrs. Lane if she had any news the following day and when she said she intended to report Mrs. Durand-Deacon's disappearance to the police, he coolly offered to drive her there himself. This he duly did and on Sunday 20th February he and Mrs. Lane reported the circumstances at Chelsea Police Station. Inquiries were instituted and it was during checks at the " Onslow Court " that Haigh's unreliability in business matters first came to light.

It was then learned at Scotland Yard that Haigh had previous convictions for dishonesty. During the ensuing days he made several statements to the police and even gave a Press Conference at the " Onslow Court " in which he aired his views on Mrs. Durand-Deacon's disappearance to a gathering of national newspaper journalists. Haigh's downfall began when the West Sussex Police were asked for their assistance. He had unwisely given his occupation as a director of Hurstlea Products at Crawley; this was untrue but it did lead to the forcing of the door of the infamous storeroom, where the revolver and particularly a receipt from a firm of cleaners for Mrs. Durand-Deacon's Persian lamb coat were incriminating items.

Even so, Haigh, though a prime suspect, might have bluffed things out a while longer, as the police had no real intimation of the true horror of the Crawley storeroom and there was, of course, no trace, in the literal sense, of the unfortunate widow. But Haigh himself, in his vanity and nonchalant belief in his omnipotence, made a fatal statement at Chelsea Police Station on Sunday 27th February, when he told police officers, " I will tell you all about it. Mrs. Durand-Deacon no longer exists. She has disappeared completely and no trace of her can ever be found again. I have destroyed her with acid."

Further sensational disclosures followed. After his appearance at Horsham Magistrates Court, where he was formally charged with the murder of Mrs. Durand-Deacon, Haigh was seen by the police in Lewes Prison where he claimed to have murdered eight other people and to have disposed of them in drums of sulphuric acid. He was under the impression that a person could not be tried for murder if the body could not be found, and in what the Press seized on, firstly as the " Acid Bath Murder " and later as the " Vampire " killings, circumstances of squalid horror were revealed.

The people Haigh claimed to have murdered by shooting or clubbing and then to have disposed of by identical means were a woman, a youth, and a girl; a Mr. William Donald McSwan in London, on 9 September 1944; McSwan's parents, Amy McSwan and her husband, about July 1945; and a Dr. and Mrs. Henderson who were alleged to have been murdered by Haigh about 28 February 1948. Mrs. Durand-Deacon was, of course, the ninth victim.

Though the police discounted Haigh's stories of the first three murder victims, it was certain that none of the McSwans or the Hendersons were ever seen again. The murderer's own confession was that he shot young Donald McSwan in a house in the Gloucester Road and then dissolved his body in sulphuric acid which he poured into a barrel. The parents of McSwan were dealt with in the same way, the motive in each case being Haigh's insatiable need for money.

His fatal liaison with Dr. and Mrs. Henderson came about when he entered into negotiations to buy their house at Ladbroke Square; the deal fell through, but after some months' friendship Haigh said he shot " Archie " in the storeroom at Crawley and later the same evening his wife; he dissolved both their bodies in acid in the same way as previous victims.

My own small connection with the Haigh affair came about when the door of the newspaper office in which I then worked was opened one afternoon in 1949. My visitor was Mr. Philip Paige, a farmer in the Sevenoaks Weald area and an amateur painter, about whom I had written a number of articles. Mr. Paige told me excitedly, " Haigh has killed my sister Amy like the others. He has put her in the acid bath."

It subsequently transpired that Mr. Paige was in fact right; though he had not seen his sister for more than twenty years she was indeed the unfortunate Amy McSwan, one of the victims Haigh had confessed to murdering. As Haigh was in fact charged only with the murder of Mrs. Durand-Deacon, the story had to be treated very carefully and the facts first given to the police.

Apart from the horror which Haigh's confessions inspired in all who heard them, more chilling detail was yet to come, and the vampiric elements in Haigh's statements were treated with incredulity by many people. The sensational stories which circulated publicly were typified by huge headlines in the *Daily Mirror*, whose then editor, Hector Bolam, was sent to prison for three months and the newspaper itself fined £10,000 with costs in March 1949, following an action by Haigh for contempt of court. The *Mirror* had carried articles and photographs naming Haigh as the vampire killer and also giving details of the missing persons, before Haigh's case had been heard and at a time when he had been charged with only one murder.

The sensation which surrounded the Haigh case may well be imagined, for not only was the detail lurid, morbid and macabre in every sense, but Haigh's next words in his lengthy Chelsea Police Station interview were to the effect that after he had murdered the six named people in his statement, he had then drunk their blood. Haigh's mentality, his background and the evidence for his vampirism, such as it is, will be dealt with in detail in the next chapter, but it would be useful at this moment to recall some of the statements which filled seasoned police officers, surgeons and journalists first with disbelief, then with mounting disgust and finally with something approaching horror.

Haigh, as we have seen, was a man phlegmatic in manner, cool and self-possessed in the tight corner in which he now found himself; but stupid and conceited in that he told many lies and made many idiotic statements which the police were soon able to disprove. Yet his dapper, even elegant air, and the poise which was to remain unshattered throughout his trial and eventual sentence, were so at variance with the squalid catalogue of sick acts he related to the police, that many people disbelieved much of a greater part of his statements.

Curiously enough, even doctors and psychiatrists consulted, if the written testimony is to be believed, were reluctant to confirm the facts of Haigh's vampirism, and his confessions, almost unique in modern criminal jurisprudence, were largely discounted. Yet they display such a disturbing wealth of sordid, not to say disgusting detail, that it is difficult to believe that they were in any way concocted. Haigh was not insane or unbalanced, though it was obvious to anyone who had anything to do with the trial that he could not be normal. And his behaviour during the proceedings was extraordinary; he remained completely unmoved by the most telling evidence against him and even affected amusement at some aspects of the prosecution's case.

The affair leapt into the international headlines as soon as the words " acid " and " blood " found their way into the public domain and it would be true to say that for many people who found even a series of acid bath murders of little interest, the mention of vampirism aroused an immediate response. Certainly, even the trial of Neville Heath or of the infamous Christie, hardly generated as much excitement.

The case of Haigh parallels in an astonishing way the traditional vampire of fiction, particularly that of Count Dracula; charming and personable, he seemed to have exerted an animal magnetism on his victims, who were mostly well-educated, middle-class people of some means. Like the vampire of fiction, he drank blood, though in this case it was that of the newly dead, not the living. The victims were sometimes killed with a revolver shot, usually through the back of the head and, as Haigh admitted to the police, he usually drew off a wine-glassful of blood and drank it to " refresh himself ".

Again, like the vampire of fiction and of legend, he showed no remorse; in fact it appeared as though the drinking of the blood fulfilled a physical need quite outside his control. He revealed a sardonic humour when contemplating the deaths of at least six innocent people. But he differed from the vampire of romantic fiction in two essential details: his motives were mainly monetary, the vampiric element, though habitually indulged in, being incidental. And, unlike Count Dracula and his ilk, he proved vulnerable to the ills of mankind and, ultimately, to their inexorable laws.

Haigh had told the police at one stage: " It sounds too fantastic for belief," and so it proved. Lord Dunboyne in his fascinating and well-argued study of the trial of Haigh in the Notable British Trials Series, makes the telling point, " No other reported case seems traceable to suggest that a murderer drank, or claimed to have drunk the blood of the murdered, as an end in itself, unassociated with any sexual perversion."

At the first two-day hearing at Horsham Town Hall, the defence and prosecution had agreed not to mention the deaths of other victims or of Haigh's reported drinking of their blood. But later, as one horrific revelation followed another, the prisoner's affirmations that dreams and "superior forces" had directed his actions, including that of drinking the blood of the murdered, were taken by the prosecution to mean that the defendant had shifted his ground and that he was attempting to appear of unsound mind when he committed the crime for which he was being tried. There was a clash of medical opinion on the point, but there could have been little doubt in the minds of the jury who took only fifteen minutes to return their verdict of guilty.

In the days when he was awaiting his trial Haigh put pen to paper and graphically outlined his early life, in which his strict upbringing and strange, unearthly dreams predominated. As a young man he became a junior organist at Wakefield Cathedral. And in his schooldays, as a solitary youngster, he spent much of his spare time there. He would sit in the fading light gazing at the figure of Christ bleeding upon the Cross.

Said Haigh, "Why not kill and be done with it and put Him out of his agony?" It was a precept he was to put into terrible practice less than three decades later. His dreams too, were filled with recurring visions of Christ and blood; the pigments were always the colour of blood. The carmine-soaked dreams of his childhood were to culminate in the vampiric nightmares of his adult life.

TWENTY-THREE

𝔙ampire or 𝔙ictim?
𝔋aigh and the 𝔅rand of 𝔖atan

THOUGH IT has long been a matter of dispute among medical circles, there is no doubt in my mind that John George Haigh was a vampire in the classical tradition, possibly the only true monster in this field in the twentieth century. By this, of course, I do not mean to imply that he was a vampire in the supernatural sense, but there is at least a strong suggestion that he needed to drink blood in order to refresh and sustain himself. It will be disgusting to many that such a creature should not only murder innocent people and dispose of them in such a revolting way, but that he should then drink the blood of the newly dead.

This is something that has to be faced in such a study and readers with a sensitive turn of mind should perhaps be warned that we are now about to turn to detailed examination of Haigh's alleged vampirism; to examine the medical evidence and to try to assess all the available facts. But first, we should know something of his earlier life and background.

John George Haigh was born at Stamford, Lincolnshire, on 24 July 1909. His father, after holding a good job as a foreman in an electricity works, was unemployed at the time, a cause of great bitterness in the family. Haigh's mother was herself 40 when he was born; he was an only child and spent his formative years at Outwood, near Wakefield, where the father then obtained work at a colliery. Haigh's solitary nature was naturally affected by his strange upbringing. Both parents belonged to a strict sect called the Peculiar People. It was aptly named; to Haigh's parents religious beliefs were of paramount importance. The growing boy was brought up on a diet of Bible parables and sayings, much of which were concerned with sacrifice. The grown man was to write later in life: " I had none of the joys or the companionship which small children usually have. Any form of sport or light entertainment was frowned upon and regarded as not edifying. There was only, and always, condemnation and prohibition." And he added, of his father: " He was constantly preoccupied with thoughts of the hereafter and often wished the Lord would take him home. It was a sin to be content with this world and there were constant reminders of its corruption and evil. Often I pondered my father's references to the Heavenly places and to the ' worms that will destroy this body '. It was inevitable that I should develop an early inhibition regarding death."

It would be remarkable, given the circumstances of Haigh's upbringing, if a normal man had emerged at the end of some twenty-five years of such formative influences as those his parents brought to bear. If Haigh's written testimony is to be trusted, his father must shoulder a great deal of responsibility for the monster who eventually shocked post-war England.

Haigh continues of his family: " So great in fact was [his] desire to separate himself and his family from the evil world that he built a great wall round our garden so that no one could look in." And he mentions a curious incident regarding the elder Haigh.

He writes: " On my father's forehead is a small blue scar shaped like a distorted cross. Explaining the mark to me when I was very young he said, ' This is the brand of Satan. I have sinned and Satan has punished me. If you ever sin, Satan will mark you with a blue pencil likewise '."

A curious conceit for a parent to display to his young son, and Haigh brooded about this for a long time; the tale of Satan's mark filled him with deep anxiety and even when, in later years, he came to realise that it was nothing but a scar caused by a lump of coal in his father's mine, he still kept looking at people in the street to see if they carried Satan's mark.

Despite the weird influences at work on his childhood, Haigh retained a deep love for his parents and he was sure they loved him also; to him they " remained all that is noble ".

Haigh went to Wakefield Grammar School and also became a chorister at the cathedral when the strict Plymouth Brethren teachings of his parents at home began to clash with the Anglo-Catholic services at the cathedral. One sinister ritual of his earlier childhood threw a crooked shadow of things to come.

Lord Dunboyne says in his introduction to the trial: " Haigh used to assert that his fond mother corrected him during childhood by smacking his hand with the bristles of a hairbrush. When his trial for murder was pending, he added that the punishment of the hairbrush drew blood, which he sucked and enjoyed to such an extent that he later deliberately cut his finger to gratify the taste he had acquired." This statement needs little comment except to note that it reinforces and helps to explain Haigh's vampirism; his addiction to blood and the blood-drinking which was to be such a feature of the trial had been a cumulative force from his early days and it does not appear to me to have been grafted on to his evidence in order to provide a basis for a verdict of guilty but of unsound mind.

Needless to say the teachings of Haigh's parents were repressive and anti-clerical and were thus basically opposed to all the teachings and influences he was subjected to at the cathedral —where he was a chorister, pianist and organist for minor services, it will be remembered.

His dreams began to assume increasing importance at this stage; the analogy of Christ bleeding on the Cross at the cathedral has already been mentioned. Haigh asserted that he constantly saw Christ bleeding in his dreams. One of Haigh's more celebrated pronouncements during his arrest and trial was that he also had a recurring dream by which he climbed to the moon by means of a huge telescopic ladder; the colours of his dreams were bloody, and the globe from his ladder in·space was also " incarnadine ", he added poetically. He also mentioned that from the age of 11 he had been in the habit of drinking his own urine.

Yet his sex life appeared normal, and he married a young girl at the age of 24. But he was subsequently sent to prison for fraud, and Mrs. Haigh disappears completely from the story; at any event he never saw her again. He had left school at 17 and after being employed by a firm of motor engineers started an advertising and estate agency. He then floated some large companies but later drifted into crime by means of fraud and forgery and was sent to prison for fifteen months in 1934. A long series of swindles and further spells in prison followed.

It was while he was in Lincoln Prison during the war that he experimented with dissolving field mice in sulphuric acid, when working in the tinsmith's shop. One wonders whether he then had any inkling of the later and more terrible use to which he was to put the idea. His obsession with blood appears to have returned when he was involved in a motor accident while working in light engineering at Crawley in the middle period of the war.

He suffered a 2-inch cut on his skull and he later said of the smash, " Blood poured from my head down my face and into my mouth. This revived in me the taste and that night I experienced another awful dream. I saw before me a forest of crucifixes, which gradually turned into trees. At first there appeared to be dew, or rain dripping from the branches but as I approached I realised it was blood."

Haigh continued, " Suddenly the whole forest began to writhe and the trees, stark and erect, to ooze blood. A man went to each tree catching the blood. When the cup was full he approached me. ' Drink ' he said, but I was unable to move and the dream faded." This extraordinary and vividly worded narrative was later somewhat discounted at the trial as being a concoction of the defendant with a view to pleading insanity.

The first true indication of Haigh's vampirism comes in his statement on the murder of the unfortunate Donald McSwan. The exact date was never established but police found in Haigh's diary, the date 9 September 1944 marked with a red cross, and it was taken to mean that McSwan met his end on that day. Haigh told the police, " I got the feeling I must get some blood somewhere. I was meeting McSwan from time to time. The idea came to me to kill him and take some blood. I hit him over the head and he was unconscious. I got a mug and took some blood from his neck in a mug and drank it . . . That night I had the dream when I caught up with the blood."

Lord Dunboyne says of this incident, " On 12th September Haigh happened to mention in a personal letter from London that he was suffering from enteritis. Possibly the complaint was caused by drinking the blood of W. D. McSwan. On the other hand, Haigh's positive statement that he was never sick after his blood-drinking casts doubts on whether he ever indulged in the habit.

because human blood, drunk neat, is almost bound to act as an emetic."

Haigh then said he murdered a middle-aged woman about November of that year, though this was never proved. But experts felt there was little doubt that he murdered both parents of Donald McSwan, and this was believed to have taken place in July 1945. Haigh said that as the father's corpse did not produce enough blood he killed the mother on the same day. The police, rather more prosaically, attributed Haigh's motives as being his desire to destroy the whole family in order to get hold of their property. All three members of the McSwan family were dissolved in acid, the same way he was later to dispose of Mrs. Durand-Deacon.

Like a sinister bird of prey Haigh then left Crawley in 1945 and booked in at the Onslow Court Hotel, some four years later to be the scene of so much excitement and police activity. But Haigh's appalling trail of crime was only half begun and soon the unfortunate Hendersons were to come within his orbit. Haigh, it is true, was keeping his hand in, it might be said, as he further confessed to the authorities that he had murdered a youth at Gloucester Road in the autumn of 1945—but this, like the reports of the other two alleged victims earlier mentioned, could not be substantiated.

Though Haigh had gained something like £6,000 through his murderous activities, by August 1947 he was again in debt. It was then that he met Dr. and Mrs. Henderson of Ladbroke Square through an advertisement of their house being for sale. He spent several months cultivating their friendship, but Christmas of that year found him ordering several carboys of acid for the infamous storeroom at Crawley. In February 1948 he ordered two 40-gallon drums. The vampire was about to claim two more victims.

It was in February that Haigh later told the police, his dream cycle recommenced. Once again, "I was seized with an awful urge. Once more I saw the forest of crucifixes which changes to trees dripping with blood. Once more I wakened with the desire which demanded fulfilment." One is irresistibly reminded of Stoker's description of Dracula's slave Renfield, who, like Haigh, was seized with the terrible urge to drink blood and who, while imprisoned, catches insects for the nourishment which they will afford his blood-lust.

Haigh continued, " Archie was to be the next victim . . . in the storeroom at Leopold Road I shot him in the head with his own revolver. I then returned to Brighton and told Rose that Archie had been taken ill very suddenly and needed her. I said I would drive her to him. She accompanied me to the storeroom at Crawley and there I shot her. From each of them I took my draught of blood."

No one ever saw the Hendersons again but Haigh's diary entries contained the initials " A. H. ", presumably for Archibald Henderson and " R. H. " for Rosalie Henderson. Haigh had followed up the entry by adding the sign of the cross. With the Hendersons dissolving into nothingness in the two drums he had bought, Haigh then proceeded to dispose of their property. He told the prison authorities that he had been impelled to kill them solely through his thirst for blood, stimulated by his dreams, and all the time he believed himself to be under divine protection. Describing the killing of Dr. and Mrs. Henderson he said, " I felt convinced there was an overseeing hand which would protect me."

So confident was he of this that when he found one of Dr. Henderson's feet still undissolved when emptying out the sludge from the drum, he left it without even troubling to hide this shocking piece of evidence within the bounds of the yard.

Haigh's next crime, his penultimate if he is to be believed, was the murder of a girl at Eastbourne; but like the earlier cases, this could not be established by the police. His dark passage through the years was completed with the murder of Mrs. Durand-Deacon the following year, when once again his debts had become insupportable.

" It was not their money but their blood that I was after," said Haigh. " The thing I am really conscious of is the cup of blood which is constantly before me. I shot some of my victims . . . I can say I made a small cut, usually in the right side of the neck, and drank the blood for three to five minutes and that afterwards I felt better. Before each of the killings I have detailed in my confession, I had my series of dreams and another common factor was that the dream cycle started early in the week and culminated on a Friday."

The investigating authorities, rightly or wrongly, tended largely to discard the vampire theory, as I have earlier indicated, but Haigh's own story—unsupported, it must be admitted—bears a powerful ring of truth and there was the significant factor of a blood-stained penknife being found in his car.

Lord Dunboyne, in a particularly interesting passage of his brilliant introduction to the trial, has this to say of Haigh's vampirism. Speaking of Haigh's statements on this factor, he comments,

He [Haigh] was well aware that humans have been known to drink blood since primeval times. The phenomenon has not been confined to the symbolism of religious ritual. It has occurred in history in other connections. About 300 BC there is an account in the Mahavagga of a certain Buddhist monk who suffered from a seemingly incurable disease. He went to a place where swine were slaughtered, and ate their raw flesh and drank their blood and his sickness abated.

Again, primitive head-hunters and warriors have been known to believe that the blood of their victims, if drunk, will engender bravery; and even during the 1939 war, it was not unknown for Colonial troops, who were stationed in Europe, to visit local abattoirs and to drink the fresh blood of sheep and bullocks for the same reason. A yet more recent throwback of a similar tradition appears in Kenya to have induced the Mau Mau initiates to lick the blood of newly slain goats.

Further, some primitive tribes have, from time immemorial, cherished the belief that by tasting the blood of a slain person the slayer will enjoy such a fusion of blood in his veins as to form a communion of friendship with his victim and avert the evils of an avenging spirit. But in such cases, the killer is usually prompted only to lick the blood, for instance from the lethal weapon, and not to drink it as Haigh claimed he had done.

[Lord Dunboyne concludes.] In all these instances, moreover, the drinking of blood is actuated by a belief in its salutary effect and not associated in any way with psychopathic behaviour. In the very rare cases of a spontaneous impulse to drink human blood, the desire has invariably been connected with a sexual perversion. Even then it has been only incidental, in the frenzy of sexual excitement. In Haigh's life, on the other hand there is nothing to suggest sexual abnormality.

[Instead, Lord Dunboyne is of the opinion.] It is probable that he [Haigh] acquired his knowledge of blood-drinking from literature he had read on the subject and that he exploited the idea in an attempt to substantiate his plea of insanity and to escape execution.

This is something which, after all, must be left to the judgement of the reader, lacking concrete evidence which would prove the matter one way or the other. Certainly, Haigh's alleged vampirism had little effect on the case; three psychiatrists called in held that Haigh was simulating insanity and that there was no reason to believe he was irresponsible on legal grounds, or insane according to the medical evidence. Haigh was therefore duly executed at Wandsworth Prison on 6 August 1949, and the greatest *cause celebre* of its kind in the twentieth century was at an end.

Was Haigh a vampire? The story unfolded in the hushed Sussex courtroom was an incredible one. It was also a macabre one, the evidence being not only shocking but disgusting to most people of normal mind. If Haigh's statements—and they tallied in so many respects, even after repetition—are to be accepted at their face value and he was a genuine vampire from a medical point of view, how much of this was his fault and how much should be laid at the door of his parents? To some people, horrible as his crimes were, Haigh must have seemed, even at the time, to be more of a victim of a unique environment, rather than a sadistic monster. This is essentially a limited viewpoint and one not likely to be held by many, but nevertheless it must be put.

Sir David Maxwell Fyfe, Haigh's counsel, in a long and cogently argued opening speech for the defence, put forward a vivid description of Haigh's dreams in support of his contention that he was a paranoic.

Sir David said: " He [Haigh] began by seeing in these dreams a veritable forest of crucifixes, and as the dream developed, in that absurd way in which even our ordinary dreams behave, the crucifixes turned into trees; in turn, one of the trees became a man. And that man appeared to be collecting something from those dripping trees. At first it appeared to be rain or dew, and as the dream developed, it appeared to be blood. You will hear that the dream repeated itself six or seven times; and the prisoner's account is that, as the blood was taken, he tried to get near to the man, but he could never get near enough to him, and he felt, first of all, an overmastering desire to have blood, and, secondly, that this controlling spirit of his was determined that he should have blood. Then, when the opportunity came to do these dreadful deeds, he felt that he was carrying out, not his own desires, but the divinely appointed courses that had been set for him in this way."

The distinguished psychiatrist, Dr. Henry Yellowlees, who was called by Sir David as one of the principal defence witnesses went exhaustively into Haigh's strange dreams. Significantly, he said of the defendant's alleged vampirism, " I think it is pretty certain that he tasted it [the blood]; I do not know whether he drank it or not. From a medical point of view, I do not think it is important, for the reason that this question of blood runs through all his fantasies from childhood like a motif and is the core of the paranoid structure that I believe he has created, and it does not matter very much to a paranoic whether he does things in fancy or fact. That is what I feel medically about it."

The important factor here is that Dr. Yellowlees said it did not matter medically whether Haigh had drunk blood or not; the witness was, of course, dealing at this point with the defendant's state of mind. Equally significantly " it does not matter very much to a paranoic whether he does things in fancy or in fact ", so Dr. Yellowlees's evidence-in-chief and his cross-examination by the prosecution, does not rule out Haigh's vampirism.

It is something which cannot be proved through the evidence produced during the trial, for there was no evidence, but as I have said before, after sifting the masses of statements made at the time, there is no doubt in my own mind that Haigh was speaking the truth. Out of his tortured childhood had emerged a malformed human being; a vampiric predator whose thirst for blood was slaked on at least six occasions post mortem. That he is an horrific figure does not preclude him from being a sad one; despite his forebears from the mists of the past, such as Gilles de Rais and Sergeant Bertrand, he remains a figure mercifully unique in the twentieth century so far.

In an age not noted for kindness or regard for human life; which has seen two major slaughters on a world scale; and the holocausts of the Nazis and the atom bomb, the vampire is still a figure which commands attention. This is the significance of Haigh and will make his case a talking point after other, perhaps more heinous crimes, are long forgotten.

TWENTY-FOUR

Nights in Highgate Cemetery

THAT THE fascination of the vampire remains a potent factor in twentieth-century life is evinced by the interest aroused by reports of vampirism—including a mass vampire-hunt by a hundred people—in the urban atmosphere of Highgate Cemetery as recently as 1970. Aptly, one of the leading figures in the hunt for the vampire was a certain Mr. Blood.

The manifestations were reported by the *London Evening News* in an article on the front page headed, " Mr. Blood in Cemetery Hunt for Vampire " which appeared on Saturday 14 March 1970. According to this report about one hundred people had joined in a vampire-hunt at Highgate Cemetery, including an expert on vampires, a Mr. Alan Blood, a 25-year-old teacher of history who had travelled from his home in Chelmsford, Essex.

The hunt followed a television interview the previous night, Friday the 13th, in which 24-year-old David Farrant had spoken of his plans to go to the cemetery to put a stake through the heart of a vampire which was lurking in the graveyard. Mr. Blood said that as a result of this he had met Mr. Farrant in a public house and they had talked about the plans. But Mr. Blood felt too many people had been engaged in the search, which would have disturbed any undead spirit.

He said he would search for the vampire himself at dawn; he was convinced that whatever was there was Satan-like in character. A great mass of people had gathered at Highgate and some of them had scaled a 10-feet-high wall round the cemetery to carry out their search. A number of them had emerged frightened and shaken and said they had seen something " crawling in the dark ". This was the promising opening to an affair which seemed as if it was out of the ordinary and so it proved. There was a brief lull and then further reports appeared in the national Press.

The new developments were detailed in the *Evening News* on 25th March of the same year, which said that Mr. Blood had held his vampire-hunt. The name of Mr. David Farrant again appeared and it was reported that he had carried out his own investigation. Mr. Farrant, whose address was given at Archway Road, Highgate, was told that a ciné club had admitted making a film in the cemetery called *Vampires at Night*, which may have started the rumours.

Mr. Farrant was unconvinced and said he felt something was wrong; four times he had seen a dark, human-like shape gliding over the ground in the cemetery and vaults had been damaged.

He told an *Evening News* reporter, " I am convinced there has been an evil spirit there."

A cemetery official was quoted as saying, " I have been here for many years and I don't believe this sort of tale. The doors of vaults are sometimes damaged but we are sure this is done by vandals. You get vandals in every churchyard. To say there are vampires here is ridiculous."

There the matter rested until the autumn and no further information was forthcoming. But on Wednesday, 30th September the *Daily Mail* weighed in with more adventures of the irrepressible Mr. Farrant, though they gave his name as Allan instead of David. Mr. Farrant was charged with entering enclosed premises for an unlawful purpose, the sequel to his romantic and van-Helsing-like appearance over the wall of the cemetery where Karl Marx is buried.

Mr. Farrant's vampire-hunt that night ended in the prosaic arms of the law as he was caught by a policeman climbing out armed with a wooden cross and a sharpened stake. But as he walked from court he commented, " I won't rest until I catch the vampire of Highgate Cemetery."

The iron-nerved vampire-hunter told the police he was looking for the bloodsucking vampire which he believed stalked the cemetery by night and slept in a coffin by day. He was sure of seeing the vampire that night—there was a full moon and he intended to follow it when it glided back through the door of a catacomb.

He told the court, " I would have gone into the catacomb, searched through the coffins until I recognised the vampire asleep in one and then I would have driven my wooden stake through the heart."

Mr. Farrant had pleaded not guilty to entering enclosed premises for an unlawful purpose—to cause damage to coffins, and the Clerkenwell magistrate, Mr. D. Prys-Jones, dismissed the case against him after a defence submission that the cemetery wasn't legally an enclosed area.

One of the most interesting aspects of the case, from the point of view of this study, is contained in the submission of Mr. Jeffrey Bays, who appeared for Mr. Farrant.

He said, " There is no evidence put forward to say that his beliefs are not true beliefs; people have spent vast fortunes looking for the Loch Ness Monster and other such serpents.

" There is no less truth in her existence than in my client's beliefs."

In the *Daily Mail* report Mr. Farrant was described as a hospital orderly and his address was then given as Manor Road, Barnet, Hertfordshire.

He told the *Daily Mail* after the case, " I founded the British Occult Society two years ago. We have about 100 members all over the country and Europe searching for vampires. We heard in February that there had been a vampire in Highgate Cemetery for about ten years. I saw an apparition one morning when I was watching the cemetery for the vampire to rise."

Mr. Farrant also claimed that the cemetery was used by a Black Magic Cult and described seeing scores of coffins that had been broken open.

Following the court case it might have been felt that the affair was closed but there was more still to come. The *Evening News* was back in the ring on Friday 16 October 1970, when they published a half-page feature of photographs, with text by Mr. Barry Simmons on the latest turn in the affair. Their five-column heading proclaimed " Midnight Vigil for the Highgate Vampire ". This time Mr. Farrant's name was back to David and he was in great form as he guided the *Evening News* reporter on a memorable night's outing among the tombs of old Highgate.

There was only one snag from a journalistic point of view. " I can't guarantee we will find any vampires," Mr. Farrant confessed.

Let Mr. Simmons's light-hearted account speak for itself. He says, in part:

> Count Dracula would have sharpened his fangs in eager anticipation as the church bells tolled midnight—the night after a full moon. The scene was set for a spine-chilling night to rival the most horrific film. Bram Stoker's Transylvania, the European kingdom of Dracula tales, had its windswept castles and creaking doors.
>
> Although there are no castles in Highgate, the ivy-covered Victorian vaults and the eerie sound of the wind in the trees helped to make up the atmosphere. David, 24, was all set, kitted out with all the gear required by any self-respecting vampire hunter. Clutched under his arm, in a Sainsbury's carrier bag, he held the tools of his trade.
>
> There was a cross made out of two bits of wood tied together with a shoelace and a stake to plunge through the heart of the beast. Vampire hunting is a great art. There is no point in just standing around waiting for the monster to appear. It must be stalked. So we stalked. Cross in one hand to ward off the evil spirits, stake in the other, held at the ready, David stalked among the vaults, past the graves, in the bushes and by the walls. When we had finished he started stalking all over again.

Though Mr. Simmons and his intrepid companion didn't actually see a vampire it made a fine, stirring article, vividly illustrated with atmospheric photographs showing Mr. Farrant poised for action with stake and crucifix at the ready, outside the darkened doorway of a great stone vault and again, in similar posture, by a stone Celtic cross marking a grave in the darkened, grass-grown cemetery. One feels that though Abraham van Helsing might have blinked a little at that Sainsbury's carrier bag and Mr. Farrant's elementary vampire-destroying outfit, he would surely have approved of his intrepid spirit.

The atmosphere was apparently enough to deeply impress the *Evening News*'s Mr. Simmons, who continues, " Only a few hours before, in the comfort of the office, it had been easy to joke about ghouls, ghosts and all manner of weird things. But as the church bells tolled midnight and David said with glee, ' This is the witching hour ', suddenly it wasn't so funny."

But Mr. Simmons's article took a more sombre turn when he added that students of the occult claimed the vampire had been haunting the cemetery since Black Magic worshippers held services there. They said graves had been desecrated and that three schoolgirls walking through the cemetery found the body of a woman which had been dragged from a tomb. The body had a stake through its chest. Members of the British Occult Society claimed to have seen black magic symbols, said Mr. Simmons.

And David himself commented, " This is no joke and people shouldn't think it funny. Black Magic circles are doing terrible things in the cemetery. I am sure there is a spectre of some kind. I saw it once. It was about eight feet tall and seemed to float above the ground."

But where David differs from the true enthusiast is in his definition of the vampire. He told Mr. Simmons, " I don't believe in vampires in the commercial sense of the word. I don't think they suck people's blood. If we see the vampire I don't think it will hurt you physically. But it will give you a horrible fright."

Certainly, extraordinary things have happened at Highgate Cemetery in the past few years, which gives the stories a certain cachet in the history of the vampire. Nearly £9,000 worth of damage had been caused at the cemetery by intruders and vandals. Graves have been disturbed, lead stolen from coffins and bodies moved. Mr. Farrant, who was sometimes joined by friends on his vigils, kept watch every night for a week after his court acquittal.

But though Mr. Simmons and Mr. Farrant, didn't actually track a vampire to its lair, Mr. Farrant remained undismayed. There was always another night and he was convinced that the vampire slept by day in the catacombs.

" He has to be destroyed. He is evil," he said.

And he added, in a tone which would have thrilled Bram Stoker himself, " There is no question of giving up. We have got to carry on until this thing is destroyed."

Epilogue

WE HAVE followed, in the course of this book, many of the dark
bypaths of the human spirit. We have seen something of how
the legend of the vampire grew from the civilisations of earlier
times to pass beyond fantasy with the monstrous crimes per-
petrated in the mist-haunted regions of Central and Eastern
Europe in the seventeenth and eighteenth centuries.

We have seen too, how the theme was eagerly seized on by the
weavers of dreams in the literary field; through Polidori and Prest
to the fantastic success of Bram Stoker's *Dracula* in the late
nineteenth century. This rich literary vein was mined by short-
story writers in the twenties and thirties of this century and
strange flowerings from Stoker's original seed are still flourishing
in the ultra-scientific age in which we now live.

The theme has been followed also in the theatre and, inevitably
in the cinema, first in the roots of the German silent cinema of
horror and latterly, with the addition of sound and colour, Count
Dracula's scarlet and black cloak streams across a thousand
screens the length and breadth of the world every day. The vampiric legend has indeed found eternal life in the celluloid of
Hammer Films, whose endless ribbons spin ceaselessly through
the cameras as old Transylvania comes to vivid reality at Bray-
on-Thames.

And lastly, we have threaded the stygian passages of diseased
minds in the casebooks of medical vampirism; have learned anew
what debasement the spirit of man can suffer in the atrocious

crimes of men like Gilles de Rais, Fritz Haarman, Sergeant Bertrand and John George Haigh.

What have we learned from such studies? That the human and the inhuman are not so far apart, perhaps? That it is but a short way from the habits of the vampire bat to the inhuman habits of the criminal vampire of *homo sapiens*. Just as it is but a short step from the killing of one man to the commissioning of gas ovens for the millions. We really should not be surprised. The waking side of life is but the reverse of the night side of nature and a very different picture is revealed, comparing the one to the other, even though but the thinness of a coin separate them.

One might ask, in conclusion: Do vampires exist? I would reply: who knows? "There are more things . . ." as Shakespeare so wisely observed. Certainly such a responsible newspaper as the London *Times* reports such events unwinkingly. I cull two at random, both of which appeared as recently as mid-1969. The first, headed, "Beware Vampires" appeared in the foreign news on 17 May 1969. The report reads, "Villagers near the West Pakistan town of Okara are reported to be sleeping indoors, in spite of fierce heat, because they believe vampires are about. They attribute recent deaths among sheep to the vampires."

The second appeared on 31st July of the same year and is headed: "Vampire Charge." This second story reads, "An elderly barber has been charged in Medan, North Sumatra, with having behaved like a vampire. He was alleged in court to have sucked the blood of two babies. The hearing was adjourned for further inquiries."

Both interesting stories, but, as is often the case, one looks in vain through subsequent issues for the sequels. This is the problem with modern reports of vampirism; the cases usually occur in remote places, as in the two quoted, and there is no follow-up which would allow the reader to learn whether the alleged vampirism was a natural phenomena or whether something more mysterious was involved.

I quote both reports, not because of their rarity—on the contrary, there are many such stories in most great daily newspapers in the course of any one year—but because they illustrate vividly the fact that the vampire is still a force to be reckoned with in many parts of the world. Legend or fact, it is something which is likely to be with us for all foreseeable time.

Though technically vampires cast no shadow, nevertheless it appears that the shadow of Count Dracula is a long one and can reach out from the dark fastnesses of the Carpathian Mountains of Transylvania even in the latter part of the twentieth century. Perhaps it is just as well that this should be the case.

At a time when men are exploring the moon and sending space-probes to the farthest stars it is only fitting that there should be some things on earth which are still unexplainable.

The legend of the vampire has thrilled countless millions at their winter firesides through the ages; long may it continue to do so.

Selected Bibliography

Dr. Fernand Mery, *The Cat* (Paul Hamlyn, London, 1967)

Dr. Montague Summers, *The Vampire: His Kith and Kin* (Kegan Paul, Trench, Trubner and Co., London, 1928)

Dr. Montague Summers, *The Vampire in Europe* (Kegan Paul, Trench, Trubner and Co., London, 1929)

Jan Neruda, " The Vampire " in *Great Short Stories of the World* (London, 1927)

E. F. Benson, " And No Bird Sings " in *Spook Stories* (London, 1928)

E. F. Benson, " The Room in the Tower " in *The Room in the Tower and Other Stories* (London, 1912)

E. F. Benson, " Mrs. Amworth " in *Visible and Invisible* (London, 1923); *Great Short Stories of Detection, Mystery, Horror,* ed. Dorothy L. Sayers, (Gollancz 1928-47)

Algernon Blackwood, " The Strange Adventures of a Private Secretary in New York " in *The Empty House* (London, 1906); various anthologies

F. Marion Crawford, " For the Blood is the Life " in *Uncanny Tales* (Benn, 1911-30, 8 impressions)

Sheridan Le Fanu, " Carmilla " in *In a Glass Darkly* (Bentley, London, 1872)

Bram Stoker, *Dracula* (Constable, London, 1897; Rider, London, circa 1947—edition undated)

Bram Stoker, *Dracula's Guest* (first published 1914; Jarrolds, London, 1966; Arrow Books, London, 1966)

John Polidori, "The Vampyre" in *New Monthly Magazine* (London, 1819; first edition, Sherwood, London, 1819)

Thomas Preskett Prest, *Varney the Vampire: or The Feast of Blood* (London, 1847; reprinted *Penny Numbers*, 1853)

Victor Roman, "Four Wooden Stakes" in *Not at Night*, ed. Christine Campbell Thomson (Selwyn and Blount, London, 1925)

R. S. Breene, "An Irish Vampire" in *Occult Review* (1905)

Augustus Hare, *The Story of my Life* (London, 1896-1900)

Drake Douglas, *Horrors* (John Baker, London, 1967)

Ivan Butler, *The Horror Film* (A. Zwemmer, London, 1967)

The Trial of John George Haigh (Messrs. William Hodge and Co. Ltd., London and Edinburgh, 1953)

Guy de Maupassant, "The Horla" in *Eighty-eight More Stories* Cassell and Co. Ltd., London, 1950)

James Corbett, *Vampire of the Skies* (London, *circa* 1912)

Jules Michelet, *Satanism and Witchcraft* (Arco Publications, London, 1958)

Edgar Allan Poe, "Berenice" in *Poe's Tales of Mystery* (Harrap, London, 1935)

H. G. Wells, "The Flowering of the Strange Orchid" in *The Short Stories of H. G. Wells* (Benn, 1927)

Sir Arthur Conan Doyle, "The Adventure of the Sussex Vampire" in *The Casebook of Sherlock Holmes* (John Murray, 1927)

August Derleth, "Bat's Belfry" in *The Midnight People*, ed. Peter Haining (Leslie Frewin, 1968)

Basil Copper, "Doctor Porthos" in *The Midnight People* (Leslie Frewin, 1968)

August Derleth (ed.) *Over the Edge* (Gollancz, 1967)

M. R. James, *Ghost Stories of an Antiquary* (first published 1910, Penguin Books, 1937)

Roger Vadim (presented by) *The Vampire* (Neville Spearman Ltd., London, 1963)

Theophile Gautier, "The Beautiful Vampire" in *The Vampire* (Neville Spearman Ltd., London, 1963)

Dom Augustin Calmet, *The Vampires of Hungary and Moravia* (Paris, 1746)

Axel Munthe, *The Story of San Michele* (John Murray, 1929)

Richard Mathieson, "No Such Thing as a Vampire" in *No Such*

Thing as a Vampire, anthology ed. Frederick Pickersgill (Corgi Books, 1964)

Sir Arthur Conan Doyle, "The Parasite" in *The Conan Doyle Stories* (John Murray, 1929)

Richard Mathieson, "Drink my Blood" in *The Midnight People* (Leslie Frewin, 1968)

Robert Bloch, "The Living Dead" in *The Midnight People* (Leslie Frewin, 1968)

Stephen Grendon, "The Drifting Snow" in *Vampires at Midnight* (Grosset and Dunlap, New York, 1970)

Cornell Woolrich, "My Lips Destroy" in *Beyond the Night* (U.S.A.)

August Derleth, "Nellie Foster" in *Weird Tales* (U.S.A.); *Not Long For This World* (Arkham House, U.S.A., 1948)

Richard Mathieson, *I Am Legend* (U.S.A.)

Theodore Sturgeon, *Some of Your Blood* (Ballantine, U.S.A., 1961)

Joris Karl Huysmans, *La Bas* (Paris, 1891)

Manuel Komroff, "A Red Coat for Night" in *Argosy Magazine* (December, 1944)

ANTHOLOGIES

Strange to Tell, ed. Marjorie Fischer and Rolf Humphries, (Julian Messner Inc., New York, 1946)

The Mammoth Book of Thrillers, Ghosts and Mysteries, ed. J. M. Parrish and John R. Crossland (The Statesman Ltd., Calcutta 1936)

A Century of Horror, ed. Dennis Wheatley (Hutchinson and Co., undated)

A Century of Ghost Stories (Hutchinson and Co., undated)

The Evening Standard Book of Strange Stories (Hutchinson and Co., undated)

The Haunted Omnibus, ed. Alexander Laing (Cassell, London, 1937)

Not at Night Omnibus, ed. Christine Campbell Thomson (Selwyn and Blount Ltd., London, undated)

The Ghost Book, chosen by Colin de la Mare (Faber and Faber, 1931)

Detection, Mystery, Horror series ed. Dorothy L. Sayers (Gollancz 1928, 1931, 1934)

Modern Tales of Horror, selected by Dashiell Hammett (Gollancz 1932)

A Century of Creepy Stories (Hutchinson and Co., London, undated)

OTHER PUBLICATIONS

Ebbe Neergaard, *Carl Dreyer*, British Film Institute, New Index Series, 1950

Dr. Hans Banziger, *Bulletin of Entomological Research*, 1969

Sight and Sound, British Film Institute publications

The Times

The Evening News

The Daily Mail

Index

C